Love Released - Book Six
Of Women Of Courage
Love Released Serial

By

Geri Foster

i

Thank You

Dear Reader,

Thank you for reading *Book Six of Women of Courage, Love Released*. I know venues are filled with many authors and books and the choices are limitless. I'm flattered that you choose my book. There are additional books in this series and if you enjoyed Cora and Virgil's journey, I hope you'll read the others.

If you'd like to learn when I publish new books, please sign up for my **Newsletter** www.eepurl.com/Rr31H. Again, I appreciate your interest and I hope you'll check out my other books.

Sincerely,
Geri Foster

Visit me at:

www.facebook.com/gerifoster1

www.gerifoster.com/authorgerifoster

www.gerifoster.com

Join us for discussion of Women of Courage @
https://www.facebook.com/groups/689411244511805/

Love Released
By Geri Foster

First Edition

Copyright 2015 by Geri Foster

ISBN-13: 978-1515188391

ISBN-10: 1515188396

Cover Graphics
Kim Killion
Lilburn Smith

Author contact information: geri.foster@att.net

This is a work of fiction. Names, characters, places, and incidents
are either the product of the author's imagination or are used
fictitiously. Any resemblance to actual persons living or dead,
businesses, events, or locales is purely coincidental.

ACKNOWLEDGEMENTS

This book dedicated to my husband, Laurence Foster. After all these years you're still my one and only love. Thank you for your support, and for believing in me when I had doubts. You've shown me that dreams really do come true and love isn't just in romance novels.

Always,

Geri Foster

CHAPTER ONE

After being married less than two months, Cora Williams didn't think she could be happier or more content. Virgil, Jack and she were finally a family. Things were going great as they were settling down into a comfortable routine.

Humming to herself, Cora reached for the coffee pot to pour Virgil a cup when a knock sounded at the door.

Pausing, she glanced at her husband. "My goodness, who would be out in this snow?"

The weather had turned miserable last night. Even with several inches of snow on the ground, Jack and his friend, Tommy, were determined to walk to school. Tommy's father, Briggs, had made the sacrifice and braved the weather.

After she filled his cup, Virgil took a sip. "Probably that mooching Earl."

Laughing, she slapped him good-naturedly on the arm. "Earl is my friend and I love him." Shaking her finger, she said, "Stop picking on him."

Finished with scolding, she put down the pot and opened the back door. Stunned, she stared at a half-frozen Pastor Charles Fuller. Ragged and unshaven, he stood on the back steps, smiling faintly.

"Please come in Reverend. Where on earth have you been?"

Holding his hat in his hand, he said, "I had to leave for a while so I could be alone."

"Take your coat off. Would you like breakfast or coffee?"

He looked so different from the man who'd prided himself on his appearance, especially at the pulpit. Thin and gaunt, his dirty clothing hung from his narrow frame like his shoulders were nothing more than a wire hanger. Glassy-eyed and distant, misery shadowed his face.

Virgil must've seen it too, because he stood and put himself between her and the minister. "Charles, what's on your mind?"

"I...I've come to make my final apology."

Virgil gave Cora a cautious look and nodded for her to move away. "How's that?"

"Miss Williams," he looked past her and Virgil to the kitchen window. "I mean Mrs. Carter. You were the one I sinned against the most."

Virgil slid over and pressed her against his back. "Why don't you take off your coat, Charles? Sit down and let's talk about this."

The pounding in Cora's chest nearly drowned out all other sounds. His obvious desperation scared her. This wasn't the same arrogant, self-righteous man who'd made her life miserable earlier. She didn't know why, but he scared her. What was wrong with the minister? Since losing his wife, Edith, he'd been suffering from depression, but today he looked lost.

An ache squeezed her heart and touched her conscience. She wanted to help. Stepping from behind Virgil, she said, "Reverend Fuller, I understand that you've endured a great loss."

Without warning, Earl burst into the room. "What the hell is going on? Who's too stupid to shut a door?" He stopped abruptly when his eyes landed on the former pastor standing in the middle of the kitchen. "What's he doing here?"

"I've come to make amends to Miss Cora."

Turning back to close the door, Earl stepped closer and shared a troubled look with Virgil. "You shouldn't be here, Charles. You need to see a doctor. You've let the tragedy of losing Edith run you into the ground."

Charles lowered his head. "I went away and talked to God. But He's forsaken me. I'm no longer worthy to preach His word or call myself one of His children."

Feeling his sorrow, Cora stepped closer to take his arm, but he yanked away from her touch and pulled a pistol from his pocket. Red-rimmed eyes, face pale, he put the gun to his temple and shouted, "I want to end it all."

Barking and growling, Pal leaped from his warm rug in the living room and dashed to the kitchen, placing himself between Cora and the troubled man.

"Quiet, Pal." Reaching down, she patted the dog on the head. "It's okay." Thank goodness Jack had already left for school.

She felt Virgil tense when he came up behind her, his body taut and ready to make a move should Fuller do anything foolish. Earl stepped back and stretched out his hands to the disturbed man.

Speaking softly, Earl said, "Charles, there's nothing that killing yourself will make right. It only leaves those behind confused and full of sorrow."

"I have to kill myself. God told me to."

Pity clogged Cora's chest. Poor man. He was so lost and alone. "Death isn't the answer."

Face contorted with despair, Reverend Fuller glanced at her. "I don't want to hurt you. I only want your forgiveness so I can go in peace."

"I forgave you long ago."

"No, she didn't," Earl shouted. "She didn't forgive you and neither have I." Earl shook his head. "I'm so unhappy with you Charles. You did horrible things that I just can't forgive you for." He pointed to her. "And you practically ruined her whole life."

"But, but I never meant..."

Virgil leaped forward, grabbed the gun and wrestled it out of Reverend Fuller's hand. He quickly handcuffed the sobbing man then headed out the door. "I'm taking him to the station."

It all happened so quickly that Cora's head nearly spun as she ran to the door. "But, Virgil, he's lost and confused."

"I know that, sweetheart. But he brought a gun into our home. What if Jack had been here? No, he's a danger to himself and others. He's going to jail and the authorities can deal with him, but he's not fit to be on the loose."

Earl came up from behind and put his hands on her shoulders. "Virgil's right. He needs help, but he can't be trusted around law-abiding citizens. He's too dangerous."

Wiping away tears, she turned and said, "But only to himself."

"That's dangerous enough. What if he'd decided you needed to die too? He could've killed all of us before taking himself out."

"I don't know. I feel so sorry for him."

"I'd have felt worse if he'd blown his brains all over your kitchen."

"What a horrible thought." How cold-hearted could her neighbor be? "He's a very troubled man."

"Damn right he is, but that don't give him the right to come into your home and kill himself. If that's what he wants to do, why come here?"

"He obviously isn't thinking straight."

"Can you imagine the aftermath that man would have caused?"

"It would've been horrible."

"And totally unnecessary, if you ask me."

"You don't think he's sincere?"

"I think he's a damned showboat."

"He was going to kill himself."

"So he says." Earl poured a cup of coffee. "If you were going to do something like that, would you come to the sheriff's house? A man who probably wouldn't allow that to happen?" Earl took a seat before being invited. "Or, if you're really going to do it, why not go out into the woods, to the church even, or take off for the wild blue yonder?"

Nibbling her nails, Cora stared at the closed door. "I don't know."

"He doesn't want to shoot himself."

"He said he did and he had a gun."

"That don't make it so."

What an ordeal. Her hands were still shaking from the ordeal. Cora didn't know what to think. She was glad Virgil managed to get the gun away from him. Hopefully, Judge Garner would decide Fuller's fate. Inwardly, she hoped he'd leave Gibbs City for good.

But, he also needed help.

At work later that day, Cora couldn't get the situation with the reverend off her mind. The sadness surrounding the situation forced her to realize Virgil and Earl had been right.

How could she ever imagine the preacher would consider taking his own life? But, he had suffered a lot when his wife died in the epidemic. Perhaps he had more guilt than grief to deal with.

The influenza had spread through the area leaving many dead in its wake. They'd lost so many people and, in some cases, whole families were wiped out. She'd tried so hard to save her patients, but there was little she could do against the raging disease.

Her thoughts went to her friend, Helen White. Her husband, Don, had been one of the casualties and it had left her heartbroken. Alone now, she still worked at the dry cleaners. With only her salary, Helen had had to move into a much smaller and cheaper house.

With her thoughts drifting to the past, Cora made a promise to stop by and see how her friends were doing. She'd been so busy there hadn't been time to visit.

As she went about her rounds in the hospital, Dr. Stan Lowery approached, worry lines etched on his face. "I just heard about Reverend Fuller. The judge called me and I suggested they have him evaluated at a mental institution."

"That's probably a good idea."

"Did he actually come to your house this morning?"

All day she'd avoided discussing the incident, but now she had little choice. "He did. Virgil was able to wrestle the gun from him, thankfully. But, he had said he wanted to end it all."

Stan leaned against the wall and put his hands in the big, square pockets of his white coat. "Why would he come to your home?" He tilted his head, he brows lowered. "I'm very worried about you."

The last thing she wanted was her good friend and colleague concerned over her. It made her uncomfortable and apprehensive. As one of the few female doctors, she had to constantly project a confident demeanor. "I don't know. Earl thinks he was trying to make a point."

"You need to be careful. If he's mentally unstable, no one knows what he's capable of."

Reliving the traumatic events of the morning tied her stomach in knots. "I just feel so sorry for him. I know what it feels like to be lost."

"We've all suffered losses and been in dark places, but we don't bring a weapon to someone's home."

Hearing her friend's opinion eased her mind. "You're absolutely correct. I just hope he gets the help he so desperately needs."

As she visited her last patient, Cora wondered if perhaps Virgil, Earl and Stan had a right to be concerned. Did the reverend intend to hurt her? The whole episode seemed strange. Could it be that his claim of suicide was only a ruse so he could get into their home and harm one of them?

As she headed toward her office, she placed her files on the counter for the nurses to update. Finally able to sit, she let out a tired breath and leaned her head back.

What a day.

Her eyes were nearly closed when Virgil knocked on her office door and entered. Smiling, she sat up straight. As he moved closer, she rose, leaned across her desk and kissed him soundly on the lips. He tasted delicious and made her heart do all kinds of strange and interesting things.

"I'm glad to see you."

Virgil laid his hat on her desk before he took a seat and looked at her. "Are you all right after this morning?"

"I admit I was a little shaken up. And I'm beginning to question the reverend's motives. Was he really there to kill himself or harm us?"

Virgil shook his head. "Beats me. I locked him up and talked to Judge Garner. As expected, he was pretty mad that Charles showed up on our doorstep."

"Stan told me he's been transferred to a mental institution." Smoothing her hair back in place, she shrugged.

"Ethan took him to St. Louis. They'll see to his needs. At least they can give him the care he deserves."

"I still can't help but feel a little sorry for him."

"Why? He made your life miserable."

"I know, but he also lost his wife."

Virgil picked up his hat and rose out of the chair. "You take care of yourself. I need to get back to the office, I'll see you tonight."

"Have you found out yet?"

Fingering the brim of his hat, Virgil looked at her with his beautiful, but troubled, blue eyes. "Her hearing is next week. They'll sentence her then."

Cora bit her bottom lip. "While we were never close, she's still my mother and I hate for anyone to go to prison."

"If I remember correctly, she shot Judge Martin in front of a lot of witnesses."

Defiance marred her words. "The man deserved it. He murdered Eleanor."

"That's a matter for the law."

Her jaw tight, Cora braced her elbows on the desk and cupped her hands. "Do you think I should go?"

"She never visited you when you were in prison. Never came to your defense either."

Ashamed of her mother's behavior and unsure what to do next, she covered her face.

"My father will survive in prison, she won't."

"There's nothing anyone can do, sweetheart. She's been convicted of murder. The state will see that justice is done."

She leaned back and looked at him. "For the longest time I worried about my reputation. Now both my parents are convicted felons. What kind of family are we?"

"You have a new family. My family and they love you and Jack as if you were their own."

She smiled and warmth spread through her body like a comfortable blanket and lifted her spirits. If she'd ever dreamed of the perfect mother, Minnie Carter would've been that person. Because she'd never had a daughter, they grew close very quickly and enjoyed being together. They'd been planning Thanksgiving dinner for later in the month.

Cora came to her feet, went around her desk and hugged her husband. "I have all I ever dreamed of."

"I live to make your dreams come true."

"Now, if Dan Martin will just leave us alone."

With her arms around him, she felt Virgil tense. She wasn't the only one who feared losing Jack. And while she had legal custody, the judge informed them that Dan could still try to take him away.

A chill raced down her spine and she shivered as her blood grew cold and her chest ached. The thought of losing one of the two most important people in her world made her skin tighten and her knees weak. No matter what she had to do, Dan would never taint Jack with his corrupt life. If he'd cared for his son, he'd never have signed the adoption papers in the first place.

Even if he regretted it now.

She wasn't a fool. Dan didn't want Jack back as much as he wanted to hurt her. After all, she'd brought down his whole way of life. Her mother killed his father, the government was investigating him on racketeering and Gene McKinnon was relentless in his intention to put Dan Martin behind bars.

But, he'd been smarter than the warden and both their fathers. There wasn't a piece of paper or a snitch that could lead back to Dan. Knowing Dan's mother, Cora suspected her of being behind all that. Dan had never shown a flash of brilliance, where his mother had always been shrewd.

Virgil squeezed her against his strong body. "Don't worry about Dan. Jack is our son and we'll raise him."

"I hope you're right."

"Trust me."

CHAPTER TWO

Virgil left the hospital not nearly as confident as he'd tried to sound while talking to Cora about Dan taking Jack. He knew the law well enough to know that courts usually think a child is better off with a parent. Even Judge Garner had warned him not to be too hopeful if Dan decided to make a case.

That's why Virgil had made a trip to St. Louis three weeks ago on business. While there, he and Batcher paid Dan a visit. He didn't threaten to kill the man, but he didn't promise not to either.

Virgil had just turned onto Liberty Street when he heard the noise of Ethan's voice travel over the radio. There was a fire in Leonard's barbershop. He hit the siren and headed downtown because every man would be needed to help fight it.

By the time he pulled up to the curb, the building had flames shooting from the upper story and smoke filled the surrounding area. Virgil found Frank and asked where he could help.

"I need you everywhere. The fire started out back, but it's spreading fast, even in this cold weather."

Virgil asked if everyone was out of the building. No one could say for sure if Leonard's wife was still inside. In the rear, he found the stairs were gone and the only way to the top floor was a ladder. Grabbing the hose, he propped the ladder against the side of the building and started climbing.

The heat of the fire made him discard his coat midway up. When he reached the window, he tried to douse the flames with water. It took several minutes before he could get the upper hand enough to climb inside the flat.

The floor beneath him felt like a sponge as he coughed from the smoke and wiped his watery eyes. Not sure he could make it across the room without falling through, Virgil called out, "Anyone here?"

"Help," in the midst of the dark smoke, Leonard's wife huddled in the corner, a rag against her mouth. She was a good ten feet away and flames and smoke impeded his trip across the kitchen. Since he weighed more than her, he called out to her.

"Patricia, it's Virgil. Crawl toward my voice."

"Sheriff, I'm afraid."

"Don't be, I'm right here waiting for you."

He inched closer to the frightened woman. He heard a noise behind him. "Don't come in here, the floor isn't that stable."

"Can you see her?" Frank's voice echoed through the roar. "Is she in there?"

"Yes, but she's afraid to move."

"You come out and let me go in and get her."

Virgil crouched down where the smoke was thinner. "I'm already halfway there. I'll see if I can make it."

He crawled on his belly, the heat from the floor burning his hands. He coughed and he drew closer. She whimpered then coughed violently. Her voice was all he had to go on because the smoke and fire were too thick.

He had to hurry or neither of them would make it out alive. Moving quickly, his hand touched her foot. He grabbed her and climbed up her body. Clutching her around the waist, he back crawled, dragging her across the floor toward the window.

The floor let out an ominous groan and Patricia screamed as she clung to him like a wet shirt. "Hold tight to my arm. Frank is only a few feet away."

Voices from below carried up to him. Patricia's husband, Leonard, screamed her name. From all the noise below, Virgil figured half the town fought the blaze.

He scooted backwards and kept going until Frank touched his arm. Virgil passed Patricia over to the fireman and they started down the ladder just as the whole floor collapsed.

Suddenly, a loud sound filled the air and Virgil had nothing to hang on to except the door frame and it was half-charred.

Dangling from the upper floor by his scorched hands, Virgil breathed relief when Ethan quickly manned another ladder, grabbed his belt and helped him down. Virgil's heart raced like a locomotive and his lungs were on fire.

He fell to his hands and knees and struggled to breathe. Even in the snow, sweat soaked his body and steam rolled off his clothing. Before he knew it, Cora knelt beside him and washed his face with a cool, wet cloth. "You damned crazy man. You almost died."

"Is Patricia all right?"

"She has a few minor burns, but she's fine and on her way to the hospital." She took his hands and examined the blisters. "You're going too."

She wrapped an arm around his waist and they both stood in the trampled snow. Looking around she called out, "Ed, take him to the hospital."

"No, I'm fine." He struggled to breathe through the coughing fits. "A little ointment and I'll be good as new."

She put her hands on her hips and Virgil knew he wasn't winning this fight. "You'll do what the doctor says even if I have to have you restrained." Angry, she glared. "You've singed your hair and there are burn holes in your shirt."

He willingly went into the ambulance without saying another word. It wouldn't do him any good. He'd learned during their marriage that it didn't pay to argue with a smart woman. A man lost every time.

After their discussion, Cora wrapped a little gauze around his palms and cleaned up a small wound on his forehead that he had no memory of getting. He motioned for Ethan to drive her back to the hospital then he returned to the site of the fire.

Frank and Leonard stood looking at the smoldering remains. Nearly everything had been destroyed. The barbershop wasn't burned too badly, but their home lay in rubble. The building no longer had a second floor.

"What happened here?" Virgil asked. "Where did the fire start?"

Slipping his coat back on, Frank looked at him. "With those fancy mittens, how are you able to drive?"

With his wrapped hands in the air, Virgil replied, "I manage."

Studying his shoes, Leonard said, "I really appreciate you saving my wife. I couldn't get to her and I was afraid I'd lost her for sure. A man doesn't realize how much he loves a woman until he almost loses her."

Knowing exactly how the barber felt, Virgil patted him on the back. "She's at the hospital. You need to be with her."

Leonard wandered through the ashes. "I'm going there as soon as I finish talking to Frank. I want to know what happened."

Frank strolled through the ashes before climbing the ladder to check out the upstairs. Only the framework remained and Virgil feared that would give way any minute.

"The fire started up here," the fireman said.

Virgil joined him. "In the kitchen," Virgil asked, "Maybe the stove?"

Wiping his face, Frank shook his head and pointed. "No, it was on the stairs. When I arrived, they were already gone and the fire had spread to the apartment."

Leonard scratched his head and yelled up to Frank and Virgil. "But what would burn in this cold? There's snow on the ground."

"I don't know," Frank replied. "But something did. That's for sure."

The Fire Chief came down with Virgil behind him. Putting his hand on Leonard's shoulder, Frank said, "Sam has agreed to take you to the hospital. There's nothing you can do here. Virgil's right, you belong with your wife."

Head down, Leonard walked to a waiting car and left for the hospital.

When the car was a safe distance away and the crowd cleared, Virgil stepped closer. "So, what do you have to say you didn't want Leonard to hear?"

Frank looked up at the burned shell of the upstairs apartment, shook his head and walked toward the fire truck. "Up there, when you were getting Patricia out, did you smell anything?"

"Besides, smoke?"

"Yes."

"Now that I think about it there was an odor, but I can't quite place it."

"Maybe kerosene?"

"Yeah, I think you're right." Checking around to make sure they were alone, Virgil narrowed his eyes and stared at Frank. "That means someone set that fire."

"That's my guess."

"Patricia could've been killed."

"If you hadn't acted as quickly as you did, she would be dead."

"Then that's murder."

"Exactly," Frank hissed.

Virgil stomped the snow from his shoes. "Who'd want to burn down the barbershop with a woman inside?"

"What about Leonard?"

Virgil lifted his chin and they stared at each other for a moment. "They've been married a long time and while they aren't the nicest people in town, I don't think either of them are capable of murder."

"If not Leonard, then who? This could've ended horribly. To kill an innocent woman is some serious concern."

A car pulled up. Judge Garner climbed out and approached. "What happened here?"

Frank shook hands with the older man. "I hate to say it, but Virgil and I think this fire was set deliberately."

"You don't say."

Virgil met the judge's gaze. "We're just trying to figure out who would do it and why. Patricia almost died."

Frank propped his foot on the running board of the fire truck. "She would've if it hadn't been for Virgil. And it wasn't a minute too soon. When he got her out, the floor fell through and we almost lost him."

Embarrassed by Frank bragging about him, Virgil looked away while the judge took notice of his bandaged hands. "What happened to you?"

"Nothing, just a few blisters and a lung full of smoke."

With the smell of wet, burned wood stinking up the area, Judge Garner slowly walked around the scene. The heat from the fire had melted the nearby snow, leaving a muddy mess behind. He didn't seem to mind his shoes getting dirty as he walked the perimeter.

He came to stand beside them. "Why do you think it was deliberately set?"

Frank took off his hardhat and tossed it in the truck. "First, it started outside the back entrance. Now, what would burn in this weather without the help of an accelerant?"

"Not much," the judge muttered.

"When I arrived, the place was in flames. Leonard had gotten his customers outside, but there was no way he could get up the back stairs because they'd already burned."

Virgil wiped his face. "I think whoever set that fire either didn't want anyone to be rescued or they didn't know Patricia was inside." Virgil wished he had a glass of water for his parched throat. "We smelled kerosene when we got Patricia out." He pointed to a large black pit. "See this area here?"

"Yes."

"If my thinking is correct, I think the person who set the fire bunched up some old clothing and put it outside the door upstairs then trailed the fire accelerant down the stairs to another pile of clothing soaked in kerosene. Whoever did it didn't try to hide the source. He just threw a match and walked away."

"That's pretty cold-blooded," the judge said, his face pale. "Do you honestly think that someone in this town would do that?"

Virgil looked around. "I don't know. We're going to have to question Leonard and Patricia to see if they had trouble with anyone. Then the other businesspeople and the neighbors." He put his hat on. "I'm hoping someone saw something."

"Good," the judge said. "You and Frank keep me posted."

As the man walked away, Virgil looked at Frank. "You're the expert here, is my guess right?"

"I think that's exactly what happened. And I want to know who would do this and why."

"You think we have an angry customer?"

"Maybe, or something more sinister."

CHAPTER THREE

Cora tended Patricia's wounds and gave her a sedative to help her rest. The woman had second and third degree burns on her left arm, her face, and most of her hair had been burned off.

As Patricia rested, her husband, Leonard, sat by her side, holding her hand. Tears coursed down his cheeks as he broke into uncontrollable sobs. What a horrible thing to happen. No one wanted a loved one to suffer and burns were the worst.

Closing the door quietly, she went to check on another patient when Stan stopped her in the corridor to get caught up on what'd happened. He was shocked that the fire had been so destructive.

"It's frightening to think those things can happen in the blink of an eye."

Crossing her arms, Cora nibbled her bottom lip. "It's horrible and she could've easily died in that blaze."

Dr. Stan Lowery put his hands in his lab coat. "I know, it's very serious. Luckily, the fire didn't spread and half the town burn down."

"I know, I guess the fire truck was there almost immediately."

"Frank is a great Fire Chief. Learned his job in the military. We're lucky to have him."

"Thank God it's over. Virgil sustained some injures saving Patricia, but getting him in to administer treatment was like trying to make a mule tap dance."

Stan chuckled. "I bet. We're very lucky to have Virgil as well. This town has a lot of heroes."

"Speaking of that, a week from Saturday, Carl Riley is getting a medal for saving us from Bart."

"That's right. Quite a courageous thing he did."

"I know, Virgil is very proud of him and the rest of us are extremely happy to be alive."

"That Bart sure had us all fooled. I never expected that kind of nonsense from him."

No one had ever discussed what Bart used to do to his employees. It would only create trouble for the employees and probably cause Nell's husband to leave her. While insisting on sexual favors made Bart a horrible man in her opinion, unfortunately it would also reflect poorly on the women.

"I worked for him and believe me, he was a terrible man. I don't miss him in the least."

"Well, for a small town, we sure have a lot of excitement."

Cora finished her day and started home. Virgil pulled up after she'd walked a block and, together, they drove home. He usually tried to be waiting for her when her shift ended, but today had been different with the fire and all the commotion.

"How was your day?" he asked. "Besides, harassing me and patching up Patricia?"

Scowling, she nudged his shoulder. "I wasn't harassing you. Those blisters could become infected and then where would you be? You couldn't take your gun out and shoot someone."

Slapping the steering wheel, he laughed then flinched. "Now you sound like Jack."

"You know that's going to be his first comment."

Outside, snowflakes the size of silver dollars fell from the gray skies and swirled on the gentle breeze.

He peered through the windshield. "I hope the weather isn't bad for Thanksgiving Day. My mom will be disappointed."

"I think we'll be able to get there safely. Jack looks forward to seeing 'Grandpa' and I don't think we'll be able to keep him away."

"Dad has sure taken a liking to the kid. They're planning to fish this summer. They'll both enjoy that."

"I'm glad Jack has a family."

He stopped in the middle of the deserted road and leaned over and kissed her. She wrapped her arms around his neck and returned the affection.

Pulling back, he said, "I love you."

"I love you, too."

He continued toward home because they were both always anxious to get to Jack. During her work days, he usually stayed with Maggie until Cora or Virgil came home. There had been a fight when she insisted on paying her friend, but Cora won out. It was only right.

Stopping in front of the house, she opened the door, stuck out her tongue and allowed the flakes to fall on into her mouth and melt. Since spending five years behind a fifteen-foot brick wall, Cora loved being outside no matter the weather.

After a few moments, Virgil ran to get Jack while she went inside to start dinner. In a few minutes, they came into the kitchen chattering about Virgil fighting a fire.

"I don't know," Jack said. "I might be a fireman when I get older. That way I could drive that big, red truck."

"That's not all Frank does. Fires are dangerous," Virgil warned. "And maybe you can go to school and just be an accountant. This way we won't worry so much about you."

Pal barked then jumped and placed his paws on his best friend's chest. Her nephew knelt down and rubbed the dog's belly. "Aw," Jack said with a scrunched up face. "That won't be no fun."

Cora went about preparing dinner. They had plenty of time to think about Jack's future. At seven, he wasn't sure about anything.

Looking at the young boy she'd grown to love with all her heart, Cora blinked back tears at the thought of losing him. For some judge to take him from her would be unbearable. How could that young, vibrant child be returned to his horrible father? The thought tightened her stomach and fear crept all over her body.

She couldn't survive that.

They'd just sat down to eat when Earl tapped on the door then entered, already removing his coat and hat. She'd set out a plate for him since he was pretty accurate about mealtimes at the Carter house.

"So, what's for dinner tonight?"

"Meatloaf."

Rubbing his hands together, Earl said, "My favorite."

"Mine's fried chicken," Virgil said with a sour look. "But as I remember, the last time we had that dish someone came over starving and practically ate the whole bird."

Earl dished up some mashed potatoes and tossed Virgil a vinegary glance. "Now, don't be getting all greedy. You have it pretty good here."

"I should," Virgil remarked. "We're married and this is my family."

"I'm family, too."

"You're a neighbor. A pesky one at that."

Putting his fork down, Earl leaned across the table. "Now you listen here, you whippersnapper. I was looking after these two long before you came along."

"Mooching is all you do."

After hearing enough, Cora held out her hands. "Let's stop arguing at the kitchen table. It's not good for digestion and it upsets Jack."

"It don't upset me," Jack remarked with a smile. "I kinda like it."

Cora frowned. "Well, you shouldn't." Her gaze went to her husband then her neighbor. "You two either be nice or leave the table."

With much grumbling, the two men returned to eating. After dessert, Jack turned on the radio for his program. She poured coffee.

Earl leaned forward. "What happened at the barbershop today?"

"Someone set the place on fire."

Clearly surprised by the news, Earl leaned back. "What?"

"Frank and I determined the fire was set deliberately."

Earl's brow wrinkled into deep furrows. "Who would do something like that?"

"Don't know yet. We're just starting the investigation."

"You think Leonard scalped someone and they got mad?"

"Surely not bad enough to put the man's wife in the hospital."

Not waiting for him to ask, Cora gave Earl a second piece of apple pie. "If Virgil hadn't saved her, there's no way she'd have made it out of there alive."

"You don't say." Earl chewed slowly. "I don't think anything like that has ever happened in Gibbs City before."

"I have to find out who set the fire and get him locked up so it doesn't happen again."

Earl took a sip of coffee. "You don't think Leonard would try to kill his wife, do you?"

"Not by ruining his business," Virgil said. "That's the only thing Leonard knows how do to. And while his shop didn't burn to the ground, there's a lot of damage because the upstairs collapsed."

Cora sighed as she pushed away from the table and began removing the dishes. "I just don't know why someone would do that. It's heartless."

"And fire is so dangerous," said her neighbor, taking his dish to the sink. "Aren't there people who just like to set fires?"

Virgil refilled the coffee cups. "Arsonists."

"Maybe we have one of those living among us."

Slowly stirring his coffee, Virgil said, "I don't know a lot about that kind of business. Before someone like that would've burned down a business, you'd think they'd have started smaller. Old, abandoned sheds, farms, stuff like that. An arsonist doesn't just decide overnight to burn down a business right on Main Street in broad daylight."

"Hum, I'll have to check this out. I have a friend in Joplin," Earl said. "He works with stuff like this. He's not really a policeman, he works for the Fire Department."

"What's his name? Maybe I can call him for advice."

"It's Fred Dawson."

"And you say he's familiar with fires?"

"Yes, some call him an expert."

"How'd you come to know him?"

"He was the one who helped me convince the council we needed a fire truck."

"I'll contact him tomorrow."

Earl wished them all goodnight and left. Cora prepared to tuck Jack in for the night. She let Pal outside for one last time before settling into the tub herself. After a bath, she returned to the couch and curled up beside her husband.

Tossing aside the newspaper, he put his arm around her and pulled her close.

"Virgil."

"Yes."

"Don't go getting yourself hurt. If there is a person going around setting fires, they'll be really dangerous. I don't want anything to happen to you."

Leaning forward, he kissed the top of her head. "Sweetheart, every day I want one thing and that's to come home to you and Jack. You're the most important thing in my life."

She cradled his bandaged hand. "Then why did you run into a burning building to save Patricia?"

She felt him shrug. "I don't know. It's just instinct."

She rose up and looked into his blue eyes. "You could've been killed."

"But I wasn't."

"You were willing to take that chance."

Virgil put his finger beneath her chin and brought his mouth down on hers. After the heart-melting kiss, he looked at her. "That's my job. I'm not willing to let someone die that I might be able to help just so I'm safe. No lawman can think like that and have any self-respect."

"But it's dangerous."

"It is, and it's my job. Don't worry. I'm careful, but I won't be a coward."

She snuggled deeper. Why did men think like that? Why didn't Virgil instinctively run away from a burning building, not into it? She worried every day might be their last.

She couldn't live without him.

They went to bed and as the house quieted down, Cora stared into the darkness. She thought of her mother, her father, Dan Martin, and all the things that could go wrong in their lives. Yet, when Virgil rolled over and kissed her ear, she forgot all her problems.

The next morning they hadn't even finished breakfast when Virgil received a call that there was another fire. He put on his coat and ran out the door.

She knew when he found out anything he'd let her know, but worrying made her morning creep by. At the hospital, Patricia wasn't in any condition to go home yet. They had her on strong pain medications and her wounds had to be dressed twice a day. Hopefully, she'd be able to leave in a week.

Leonard remained at her side, ignoring any attempt to get him to take care of his business or try to salvage what he could. He only wanted his wife well and out of the hospital.

"Leonard, where will you and Patricia go once she's released?" Cora asked.

"Her sister lives in town. She's going to put us up for a while. Until the insurance company pays."

"You have a fire insurance policy?"

"I almost didn't. But, Mike Huckabee opened an insurance company three months ago and he talked several of us business owners into buying a policy in case something like this should happen."

"I didn't know you'd purchased a policy."

"I don't know how good it is. Mike said the damage had to be assessed and then he'd file a claim with the head office."

"I hope everything works out for the two of you. This has been a horrible ordeal."

"You're right, Miss Cora, it has, but I appreciate all you've done for my Patty."

"She'll recover, but there will be scars. And let's hope no infection sets in."

"I've been praying the whole while."

Cora thought of Reverend Fuller and wondered if the man would've been able to help the Caseys. Perhaps they'd get a new preacher. The town sorely needed a man of God now.

CHAPTER FOUR

Virgil entered the hospital but he wasn't there to see his wife. He'd come to talk to Leonard. They hadn't had much time yesterday, now Virgil had to get to the heart of the matter.

Gently knocking on the door before entering Patricia's room, he found her husband sitting at her side, his head bowed. "Leonard, do you have a few minutes for some questions?"

The barber jumped to his feet. "Yes, of course. Have you found out anything yet?"

"Frank and I suspect that someone deliberately set that fire."

"What?" Leonard's eyes grew wide and his mouth gaped open. "That's not possible. No one would want to hurt my wife. She's a kind, God-fearing woman."

"We don't know that the intent was to harm Patricia. But maybe you had an angry customer or someone mad enough at you to do something like this?"

Leonard held out his hands and shook his head in denial. "I can't think of a single person who'd set fire to my business or my home." His brown eyes pleaded. "It just can't be."

"All the evidence points to arson."

"But, why?"

"I'm hoping you might have some information to share."

"Like what? I was in the shop cutting Arthur's hair when I smelled smoke. I had a couple of customers waiting so I just figured Patty had burned something in the oven."

"So you knew it came from upstairs?"

"Well, I assumed it had because everything, including my fuse box, is in open sight in my barbershop. There's nowhere a fire could hide."

"When did you call Frank?"

"Arthur said something to me about the shop filling with smoke. That's when I looked up and saw the ceiling smoldering. Then I knew the upstairs was on fire. We all ran out the building. I went out back to use the stairs to get Patty, but they were already burned up."

"The stairs caught on fire and you didn't smell it sooner?"

"I recently installed a new door, so it was almost airtight. I did it because the cold draft had the customers complaining."

"Did you notice anyone hanging around, hear anything?"

"No." He shrugged. Just regular Main Street traffic. I'd been busy all day so I wasn't paying a lot of attention to what went on outside the shop. I put my closed sign up around noon and went upstairs and had a sandwich with Patty."

"What time did you come back down?"

"About an hour later. Arthur had called me to say he'd be in around two and I didn't want him to have to wait long."

"But the fire didn't start until about three."

"He was running late. Called to say he was tied up with something at one of the mines and he'd be by later."

"So, there's no one mad at you and you didn't see anyone?"

"That's all I can say, Sheriff." Leonard looked back at his wife. "One of the nurses said there was another fire."

"There was this morning. It turned out to be a controlled burn at the old dairy. We'd been told about that one, but Frank wanted the fire truck there should it get out of control. People saw the flames and panicked and called it in."

"The old Hofstede Dairy?"

"Yeah, they decided to torch it rather than take the time to tear it down. They start construction on the new building next week."

"Who's going to be delivering milk?"

"They will, it will just be fresh off the farm."

"They'll have to decrease production."

"Apparently, the building was ready to fall down and was eaten up with carpenter ants. So, he had no choice."

"I wish he'd been able to buy up one of the buildings standing empty."

"A dairy wouldn't be an ideal business on Main Street. They have a lot of traffic and equipment. They're in a good location."

Leonard walked to the window and looked out. "I see Carl and Buford's gas station is doing well."

"I think they'll make a go of it. Eddie Summerfield and his sons probably don't like it, but nothing wrong with a little competition."

"Yeah, my guess is some barber from Joplin or a nearby city will move in and open up shop."

"Why don't you do that?"

"I have to wait for the insurance money."

That surprised Virgil. Most people considered having insurance a real luxury. "You have a policy?"

"Bought one, but I'm not counting on much. As soon a Patty gets out of the hospital, I'm going to try to get my shop back open." In frustration, Leonard brushed back his hair. "I hate to lose that building. My nephews are over there going through the place to see what can be salvaged."

"I'll check in later."

Going in search of Cora, Virgil passed a few nurses and Dr. Lowery, who stopped and shook his hand. Desperate to reassure his wife that the fire wasn't serious, he found her in the cafeteria and joined her for lunch. Hospital food wasn't any better than Betty's, but they enjoyed a sandwich.

"I'm so glad there wasn't another suspicious fire set. That's frightening and will make the whole town uneasy."

"I'm meeting with Earl's friend this afternoon. He's coming to town to look at the site."

"Leonard told me he had some insurance. You don't think he'd burn the building down for the money, do you?"

Virgil shrugged and took a sip of his coffee. "Depends on how much money we're talking about. But, I don't think he'd put his wife in danger."

"I agree with you. I've been trying to get him to go home and get some rest, but he's reluctant to leave her side."

As his heart reached out to her, he covered her hand with his. "I'd be the same way."

She graced him with one of her beautiful smiles that made it really hard for him to think straight. "I know you would, but it's not practical."

He leaned back and hooked his thumb around his belt. "Now, remind me again, who wouldn't leave me in the hospital when I was shot?"

Blushing, she lowered her pretty face and stared at her lap. "That's different, I'm a doctor and I wanted to make sure you were getting the right kind of care."

"You said Dr. Sam was the best there was."

Her cheeks turned a brighter shade of pink. "He is, but a second opinion isn't a bad thing." Her lips twitched slightly. "Besides, who would you rather have holding your hand? Dr. Sam or me?"

"When you love someone, you want to be with them when times are difficult. It's just normal."

"Well, today I'm insisting Leonard go home and get some rest. Besides, Patricia is getting much better."

"When he leaves, call me. I want to talk to her when Leonard isn't in the room."

"Really? Do you think he started it?"

"I don't know and it's my job to find out. If he thought she was out or something." Virgil shook his head and stood. "It's part of the job. You have to ask the hard questions and you have to assume the worst."

Virgil left to meet up with Fred Dawson. He was a nice looking man, but a mite young to be a friend of someone Earl's age. However, he carried the title of Lieutenant. Matching him in height, Dawson had keen eyes and a stillness about him that spoke of intelligence.

"I wish I'd known about you earlier. I would've called yesterday."

"That's okay," said Dawson. "Once the flames are gone, that's when I go to work." Squinting, he looked at Virgil. "What do you think happened?"

Virgil explained his and Frank's theory. The Fire Chief had joined them since the dairy fire was out and there was no hint of danger left.

"I agree that the original ignition site was right here." Using a broken branch, Dawson pointed to where the bottom step would have been. "Whoever did this used a lot of accelerant because the fire had to jump up each step and that's not easy to do. So, my guess is the person was running at full speed down the stairs, pouring out a lot of fuel to make sure the fire was big enough."

"That's a lot of weight for a person running."

Pushing back his hat, Dawson looked around. "And he'd have to escape through here to keep from being seen with some kind of a can." The investigator bent down and picked up a charred piece of wood. "Unless the can's inside."

"You think he threw it in the apartment?"

"I don't know, but can he take a chance of being seen running away from a fire with a container of kerosene? Someone would've noticed."

Staring at where the upper apartment once stood, Virgil stroked his chin. "What if he set the fire down here then ran up the stairs with the can of fuel. With the fire chasing him, he pitched the evidence inside the house and jumped down."

Looking up, Frank said, "That's quite a distance."

"Not for a young, healthy man. The snow would've helped cushion the jump."

They looked to Dawson who stepped back to get a better look at the damage. "It could have gone either way. Did you find an empty can up there?"

Frank shook his head.

Glancing behind them, Virgil started walking toward the buildings separated by an alleyway. There was a row of warehouses used for storage by various businesses. With Dawson beside him, Virgil looked for a discarded can. It wasn't in the first block. They moved to the second area which was a neighborhood with houses. On the corner, behind a shed of the Livingston's house, Virgil spotted a red and yellow can for motor oil.

He called Dawson over. "I think we found what we're looking for."

The Lieutenant looked around. "So, he ran two blocks before getting rid of the evidence."

Climbing over the fence, Frank looked back. "Probably figured we'd check the warehouse first."

"But, how long would it take for someone to find a brightly colored can?" Dawson asked.

Virgil took the evidence that Frank handed him. "He really wasn't trying to hide anything."

"His first mistake was that we wouldn't assume it was arson to begin with. After all, most homes catch on fire because of a cigarette, an unattended lamp, a candle, the oven, or a fuse box catches on fire."

Bouncing over the fence, Frank asked, "You think whoever did this didn't count on us figuring out immediately that this wasn't just an accident?"

Shaking his head, Dawson looked back toward the burned building. "I can't say that this is the work of an arsonist. Not unless there are more fires. But the person who set this fire thinks they're pretty smart. Smarter than the law and the Fire Chief."

"I think we should ask the citizens around here if they saw anything," Frank suggested.

"If they did," Dawson said, "Wouldn't they have already said something?"

"People in this town tend to mind their own business." Frank wiped his brow. "And it's not unusual for a man to be walking around town with a five gallon can of kerosene."

Dawson looked doubtful. "Even after a fire?"

"Most people don't know that we suspect this fire was set. They're all assuming Patricia was baking something in the oven then fell asleep on the couch and the fire started that way."

Virgil stepped forward. "I think we just have to wait and see what comes out of this. I did learn that Leonard has insurance on his business."

Frank touched Virgil on the arm. "Don't fault him for that. It's partly my fault. I encouraged the business owners to protect themselves against just this sort of thing. How many times have we gone to a fire and watched as people lost everything they own? It sometimes takes them years to get back on their feet."

"He's right," Dawson said. "More and more people are getting insurance. We can't use that as a motive. It appears Mr. Casey had a good business here without competition. Why would he destroy his livelihood?"

Not knowing frustrated Virgil and made him clench his jaw. "Maybe he wants to start a new business."

"He could probably sell that building and make more money than he will with insurance," Frank said. "It's not a get rich quick thing."

Dawson had to get back to Joplin. "Let me know if anything else happens." He held up the container. "Meanwhile, I'll check for fingerprints on this, but it's a long shot I'll find anything useful."

As he drove away Virgil and Frank stood staring at the rubble.

"This is a crime," Frank said. "I hate to see this. And to think someone deliberately tried to burn down a building sickens me."

Virgil let out a breath. "Yeah, me too. We can't have this kind of thing going on or our citizens will become afraid to sleep at night."

"Yeah, I think we need to talk to the judge because you might need more deputies."

"I can't get over this happening in the middle of the day." Virgil walked toward his car. "I'll be glad to put this bastard behind bars."

CHAPTER FIVE

Cora arrived home from work and found Tommy and Jack inside playing a board game. Maggie stirred something in a pot. "That smells delicious." She followed her nose to the kitchen.

"I thought I'd fix a double batch of soup and we'd split it," Maggie said, taking a sip from the wooden spoon. "The boys wanted to stay here to play games, so I thought I'd cook while keeping an eye on them."

"I'm so glad you did. That keeps me from having to fix dinner tonight."

Maggie smiled as she continued to add ingredients. "Also, it kept the two of them from catching pneumonia, because they really want to be outside playing."

Cora rubbed her frozen hands together. There were at least two inches of new snow since morning. "It's too cold."

"They don't seem to mind that one bit."

Removing her coat and laying it over the back of a chair, Cora pulled out a bowl to mix up cornbread. "How is Briggs' job going?"

"Real fine," Maggie said with a smile. Since her husband, who'd been injured in the war, didn't have to work in the mines anymore, the whole Cox family was grateful. "The bank manager is very pleased with his work. He's thinking of making him a district manager."

Cora loved it when good things happened to those who deserved it. "That's wonderful news."

"I've asked him not to take it. He'd be traveling most of the time and we have three boys who need a firm hand."

Cora thought about that and how lonely Maggie would be. She'd hate for Virgil to be away any more than he was. "I don't blame you one bit."

Maggie looked at her and raised a brow. "It'd be more money."

Cora hugged her friend. "Money isn't everything. Being a good solid family is."

"I think you're right. My boys respect and look up to their daddy. I don't want that to change."

"Nothing can because Briggs is a good man through and through."

Maggie smiled as she poured half the soup into a pan. "I think you're right."

"Is he still helping Carl and Buford?"

"He is, and he told me last night at supper that they were going to show a profit this week."

Cora clapped her hands and pressed them to her mouth. "That's the most wonderful news."

"I always like to see the underdog win."

"Me, too." Cora slid one pan of cornbread into the oven and moved the other, to be cooked later, closer to Maggie. "Are you going to the big celebration next week when Carl gets his medal?"

"Wouldn't miss it for the world."

Maggie called Tommy and together they darted across the street to their house. Smiling over Briggs' success, Cora couldn't wait to share the good news with Virgil. She'd just changed clothes and wrapped an apron around her waist when he came home.

She'd seen that look before. Something was troubling him.

As Pal ran for his usual scratch behind the ears, Cora asked, "Nothing new on the fire?"

"We found a few things, but none of it will lead us to who set it."

"Hi, Uncle Virgil." Jack ran and threw his arms around Virgil's neck. "You shoot anyone?"

Virgil put him down and held up his still bandaged hands. "Sorry, another slow day."

"You gotta catch more robbers and shoot 'em like they did Bonnie and Clyde."

"We don't need that kind of trouble around here." He ruffled Jack hair. "You do understand that my job is to keep the peace, don't you? That means I try not to have to shoot anyone."

"Yeah, but that sure is boring."

"I think you've been listening to too many programs on the radio."

Jack's face turned cloudy. "I like the radio."

Taking the young boy by the shoulders, Virgil spoke quietly. "It's okay, but remember it's not real life."

"I know." His face lit up. "Hey, guess what. I'm going to be an Indian in our Thanksgiving play. There won't be any cowboys, though." Jack let out a disgruntled sigh and shook his head. "I'd rather be the Lone Ranger."

"I'm sure you'll be a terrific Tonto. Now go on and get washed up." Jack turned and ran into the bathroom patting his hand to his mouth, doing his war cry imitation.

Virgil moved over to kiss Cora then he buried his nose in her neck. "Something smells delicious."

"Maggie made soup."

He raised his head and their gazes met. "I wasn't talking about food."

She slapped him gently with a dish towel and asked him to set the table. "And be sure and put out a place for Earl."

"That guy's a pest," Virgil said, then swatted her on the behind when she bent down to take the cornbread from the oven.

Startled, she jumped and rubbed her backside. "Ouch." She straightened and put the hot pan on the table. "He's lonely and I think the only time he gets a decent meal is when he eats here. Besides, he'd been a good friend to us."

Virgil reached up and took the plates from the cupboard and returned to the table. "Well, he shouldn't have run off Miss Winters."

Cora paused and tried to figure out when exactly things had turned in the older couple's relationship. Miss Winter had been hired to help Earl after he caught the flu and for a while they got on nicely. Cora and Maggie were waiting for wedding news any day. Then the next thing they knew, the elderly woman packed her things and returned home. "I don't know what happened there, but he's all alone again."

"I don't blame her one bit. He probably made her miserable."

Cora loved Earl and she didn't like when Virgil picked on him. However, most times she overlooked what was said because anytime Earl needed something done, Virgil was the first person on the scene. "Well, don't let Jack hear you. He wouldn't understand and he loves Earl, too."

"You're right, I'm just tired and my hands hurt. But the man can be a pill sometimes."

Turning her head so he couldn't see her grin, Cora ladled out the soup while Virgil cut the cornbread then said, "He isn't the only one."

They waited a few minutes for Earl to show up, but when he didn't, Cora assumed he was napping and would drop by later for leftovers.

They finished dinner and Virgil received a call about a car accident on Broadway. Ethan was there, but obviously it was very serious. Since it wasn't her night for emergencies, Cora cleaned the table and went through her nightly routine.

Just as she was ready to take her bath, Earl tapped on the back door. Since a break-in earlier, she kept the doors locked when she and Jack were alone.

Pulling her sweater tighter, she said, "You're late tonight. Let me warm up some soup."

"No, I'm not hungry. I ate over at Maggie's tonight. Her oldest boy is doing some work for me around the place and Maggie came to get him for supper and invited me to join them."

"Well, that's nice. And you didn't miss a thing because Maggie made enough soup for all of us."

"It was pretty good."

She poured him a cup of coffee then pulled out her usual chair and sat at the table. Determined to get to the heart of the matter, she asked, "Tell me, what happened between you and Miss Winters?"

"Nothing, 'cept she wanted to get hitched and I ain't gonna do that."

"Why not? Wanda's been gone a long time. You could use the companionship."

"I don't need a wife and I don't like her company."

Cora blew on her hot coffee. "She's very nice."

"We've been through this before. I don't like her."

Shaking her head in disgust and impatience, Cora held out her hands. "I can't imagine why."

"I just don't and I ain't marrying the woman."

"I think you make a nice couple."

"I think she's a pain in the ass."

That was Earl being stubborn. He could sum a situation up in a few words. Laughing, Cora realized the relationship was over. Earl might be a lot of things, but he always spoke his mind. "I think you don't like the fact that Meredith is her sister."

"I don't care that she's her sister. I told her not to come back around."

Ducking her head and sipping on her coffee, Cora scowled. "That was rude."

He pointed his finger and narrowed his eyes. "Now listen, I don't beat around the bush with anyone. I told her I didn't need her help and she could stop coming by. Well, she kept showing up every single day until I had to come right out and tell her to get out and don't come back."

41

"That hurt her feelings."

"I tried to be nice, but she's thick-headed as a goat." He took a sip of coffee. "I hate someone who can't take a hint."

"Your hints are rather brutal."

"Well, she's gone and I don't want her back."

"I don't think you'll have that problem in the future."

"Good. Now where is Virgil?"

"There was a wreck close to downtown. He's meeting Ethan there."

"Hum, must be serious."

"I imagine. The roads are really slick."

"I'm betting it snows on Thanksgiving Day."

"I've been meaning to ask. We're going to Virgil's parents' for dinner that day. Would you like to join us? Minnie said to invite you."

"No, I'm fine. I already have plans."

That was a surprise. Not every door in Gibbs City was open to Earl Clevenger. As a matter of fact, few were. "Where will you have the holiday?"

"Oh, don't worry, I'll be fine."

"Will you be alone?"

He frowned. "No, I'll be with friends."

She narrowed her eyes. "What friends?"

"You think I ain't got people who care about me?"

"I know you Earl and if you spend the holiday alone, I'm going to be very upset after I've invited you to be with my family."

He smiled. "I won't be alone."

"But you won't fess up, either?"

"That's right." Earl stood. "Well, I better get home. I need my beauty rest. A man's got to take care of himself."

He left Cora smiling. He'd come to mean the world to her and she could only imagine the things he'd done to make her life easier. Beneath that prickly attitude, he really cared about the people of Gibbs City.

After tucking Jack in, she enjoyed a leisurely bath, something she seldom had time for lately. When she finished and opened the door to the steamy bathroom, she discovered that Virgil had come home. Tying her robe, she glanced up and saw him. His face was pale and drawn with fatigue, or something else.

Grief.

"Was it a bad accident?"

"Yeah, a family, a father, mother and two youngsters around Jack's age."

She walked over to him and put her hands on his chest. "What happened?"

"Some drunken farmer from Carterville on his way home from the honky tonk swerved over into their lane and hit them head on."

"Were they killed?"

"Yes. All dead before the ambulance got there."

"What about the farmer?"

"He's in jail sleeping it off."

"How horrible. You sit down and let me pour you a glass of whiskey."

His brow practically touched his hairline. "Where'd you get liquor?"

"Dr. Lowery goes to Kansas once in a while and brings back a bottle or two. I asked him to get me one."

"Bringing liquor across the state line?"

"I didn't ask any questions. Besides, it's not illegal for us to have liquor in our home and you need a drink." She winked. "Doctor's orders."

Without letting him reply, she poured a small glass while he hung up his coat. They sat on the couch and Virgil accepted the glass of golden liquid. He sniffed the contents and looked up at her with a grin. "Expensive."

"Well, it's not bathtub gin."

"Are you going to join me?"

She poured herself a small drink and returned to the couch. They touched glasses in the air then took a swallow. It was smooth and fiery at the same time.

"That's good stuff," Virgil said, his lips puckered.

She smiled. "I'm glad you like it. I got it for occasions like this. There are times when everyone can use something stiffer than homebrew."

He drained the glass and handed it to her. "I agree."

"Do you want to stay up for a while?"

"No, I'm tired." He looked at her. "Although I might be able to muster up a little energy." Leaning over to nuzzle her neck, he sniffed. "Um, you smell like flowers."

She giggled, took his hand and led him into the bedroom. "That's my new lotion. I'm glad you like it." Moments like this, Cora enjoyed being married. Sharing her life, the small burdens, and the calm goodness of a small house filled with love. It made her heart happy to love Virgil and she was so thankful he loved her in return.

Cora had just fallen into a hard sleep when the phone in the living room rang. Tossing aside the warm covers, she padded barefoot on the cold floor to the phone. "Hello?"

"It's Frank. Newman's Feed Store is on fire."

CHAPTER SIX

When Cora woke him, Virgil practically threw on his clothes and then he almost ran out the door without his coat. Dashing to the squad car, he nearly slipped and broke his neck. Firing up the engine, he turned on the siren and headed downtown.

The place was lit up like the Fourth of July. Amid the chaos, Frank stood off to the side watching the building burn. Everyone huddled at quite a distance from the building. Men milled nervously by the fire truck and down the block. "Where's the hose?"

Frank grabbed his arm to prevent him from moving closer. "We can't get any closer."

"Why?"

Pointing to the inferno, Frank's voice cracked harshly, "The building is full of ammonia nitrate."

"Oh, hell."

"Yeah, the place is too dangerous." Frank took Virgil by the elbow and moved away from the crowd. "It gets worse. He also has dynamite in there for the mines. So get ready for some noise."

Just as they turned, the building exploded several times, shaking the very ground they stood on. Memories of a different time ran through Virgil's mind and he fought to stay in the moment. Since the war, he'd been avoiding loud explosions. They instantly swamped him with the nightmare of the battlefield where he was surrounded by dead bodies.

Frank gripped his shoulder and the next thing he knew, Carl was on his other side. "Just hold on, Virgil," Carl said. "You're right here in the good old US of A."

Virgil swallowed and the bile in his stomach churned as the smell hit him full force in the face. Trying to clear his head, he staggered backwards, but didn't go far because his friends held on to him.

After several minutes of Carl talking and him not hearing a word, Virgil was able to open his eyes and look around. Before him was a smoldering heap of debris. There wasn't a single recognizable part of Newman's Feed Store left. Not a thing.

Shelby Newman stepped over to them, his hands trembling. "My God, how did this happen?"

Frank let go of Virgil and put his arm around Shelby. "I got a call about twenty minutes ago that Mr. Pennyworth was working late at the mining office when he saw flames coming from your building."

"How on earth did it catch fire? I was so careful."

"We don't know yet, but we'll be investigating. There's not much you can do here. You might as well go on home and be with your family."

"No, I'll stay and help with the cleanup." He watched intently as the volunteers hooked up the fire hose and began extinguishing the flames.

Virgil stepped closer. "There won't be an immediate cleanup. There will be a guy coming from Joplin. He'll be able to tell us what started the fire."

Shelby Newman was a short, stout man with a handlebar mustache and a full head of gray hair. He'd been in Gibbs City as long as Virgil could remember. His wife used to teach school, but had decided to retire a few years back. "You think someone set this fire?"

"We don't know. But we're not taking any chances."

Shelby looked down the block at the burned out barbershop. "You think these two fires were set by the same person?"

"We don't know that and we don't want a town full of hysterical people worrying about a serial arsonist. We'll get to the bottom of this."

"Dear God, help us all."

Virgil stayed on the scene the rest of the night. Meredith had come to them with hot coffee and some kind of muffins. All Virgil wanted was something hot to drink. He needed to stay awake. Dawson would be there any moment and he wanted to go over the crime scene with him.

As daylight broke the horizon, Virgil, Carl and Frank sat on the bumper of the fire truck and sipped more hot coffee. From the water spray and the cold weather, icicles had formed on their hardhats so they tossed them in the rear of the vehicle.

Shivering from the freezing temperatures, puffs of cold air spewed out of their mouths as they spoke. "This is a helluva mess," Carl said. "First the barbershop, now the feed store."

Frank threw out the grounds in the bottom of his cup. "We've got to find out what's going on."

"I asked Dawson to get here as soon as he could. Pennyworth is waiting. I want Dawson to ask the questions. We now know we're up against something big."

"I agree," Carl said. "Every businessman in the area is going to have to be watchful if there's a maniac out there running around burning down businesses."

Frank rubbed his forehead. "My concern is what if this guy gets tired of businesses and moves to homes? Then we have people's lives at risk."

Dawson drove up and they walked over to meet him. He tossed his hat in the back seat and pulled out a hardhat. Dressed in coveralls and heavy boots, he moved toward the store. "Was this blown up or set on fire."

Frank turned to face the detective. "That was a feed store. It stored ammonia nitrate and dynamite."

"That explains the explosion." Dawson moved closer, walking into the rubble. "The problem is, since it blew up, it probably destroyed any evidence left behind."

Virgil rubbed his face. "I was afraid of that."

"But, let's keep looking. The most likely place will be in the rear of the store where the arsonist wouldn't be detected. He was sloppy before, maybe we'll find something."

They moved through the empty shell of the store to the back where not even the frame of the door remained.

Shelby caught up with them. "Have you found anything?"

Virgil introduced the owner to Dawson and they shook hands. "What time did you close?"

"Seven, I always have a late dinner waiting for me at home."

"Notice anything throughout the day?"

Shelby scratched his head. "Nothing that comes to mind."

"No one prowling around the back?"

"I have a delivery boy who usually is out there, but he was off yesterday because his mother had to drive his father to Joplin for some legal business."

"You trust this kid?"

"He's been with me since he was fifteen years old. That's about seven years. Good boy. His father on the other hand is nothing but trouble."

Dawson turned to face Shelby. "How so?"

"He drinks too much and he's not that good to his family. Takes every dime Roland makes."

"Did the dad have anything against you?"

"No, I rarely see him. And when I do, I don't say much." Shelby looked around at the charred remains of his business. "Besides, destroying my business just cost his son a job."

Dawson put his hands in his pocket and turned to Virgil. "You said there was a witness."

"Mr. Pennyworth called in the fire. I don't know if he saw or heard anything."

"Let's find him."

A block away, Pennyworth sat in his small office completely surrounded by papers and ledgers. He looked up when they entered and took off his wire rimmed glasses. "What can I do for you?"

Virgil stood directly in front of the accountant. "We're here because a couple of guys out there said you might have seen or heard something last night."

"I thought I heard a man running down the street about twenty minutes before I noticed the fire."

"What kind of sound?" Dawson asked, "Loud footsteps, fast, or clumsy?"

"No, this person was fast as lightning. He ran like a bat out of hell."

"Did you find that unusual, Mr. Pennyworth?" Virgil asked. "Someone out so late, running."

"I did find it strange. I got up and looked out, but I didn't see anyone. They'd already passed my window."

"Then nothing until the fire?" Frank asked.

"I went back to work. We're having an internal audit today and I have several things to get in order. There was so much to do, I had no time to really pay much attention to what went on outside."

Dawson took off his helmet. "When you first noticed the fire, where were the flames coming from?"

"I saw them through the large plate glass. Fire was inside the building."

"So, the outside of the building wasn't on fire yet?"

"Maybe in the back, but I couldn't see there." Taking out a pristine handkerchief, he rubbed his glasses then hooked them over his ears. "Shame about the feed store. Shelby's a good man. I hope you catch the bastards who did this."

The four men left, following Dawson to the site. "My guess is they broke in, set something inside on fire then left through the front door."

Looking back, Virgil asked. "You mean, he lit the place up and just walked out like he was minding his own business?"

"Whoever set this fire had to know about the ammonia nitrate and dynamite. They gained access through the back door to prevent being noticed and less chance people would hear any noise. But once the blaze was set, he didn't retrace his footsteps. He just opened the front door and took off running." Looking at the damage, Dawson continued. "I doubt he even bothered to close the door behind him."

"The shock waves from the blast blew out the doors and windows," Virgil said. "Once it exploded all evidence went up in smoke."

"Virgil is right. But, if Pennyworth heard a man running, he probably wasn't slowing down to turn corners, which, if he left through the back he would've had to do. I say he lit the fire and hit the front door at a dead run."

"You could be right." Virgil looked around. "I don't see an empty can around here."

"He probably didn't need an accelerant because, in a feed store, there's a lot of stuff that will ignite quickly. Also, it was inside where the weather wouldn't affect the damage the fire could do."

Virgil shook his head. "I can't believe someone just walked in here, set the place on fire, and ran away."

Dawson headed toward his vehicle to get his camera. "I'm going to continue to search the debris." He turned back to Virgil. "Try to find someone who'd do this. They probably live in this community. There has to be something that links this to your business community."

"I'll spread the word to the townsfolk to be aware and take note of what's going on around them."

Carl spoke up. "I'm staying at my gas station with a shotgun. Anyone comes near my place, they'll be sorry."

"That might not be a bad idea." Dawson got in his car. "I'm going to get some breakfast, then I'll be back here after that."

"I'm checking in with my family," Virgil said. "Frank and I will meet you here later."

After the investigator left, Virgil turned to Frank and Carl. "What do you think?"

"I don't think he'll find much here. All the evidence was destroyed in the blast. But I do agree with the things he said."

Carl scratched his head. "I'm not sure you're going to learn much here. But I think all the business folks need to watch their stores. If this keeps up, people will start to panic."

"I'm going to stay on this, but between the three of us, we need to come up with some suspects. I'm calling Ethan in to do background checks on anyone we suspect."

CHAPTER SEVEN

Cora had left Virgil's breakfast warming in the oven before leaving for work. She had no idea what had happened last night, but she felt sure she'd learn at the hospital. And she was right. No sooner had she stepped into the building than the staff started discussing the explosion and fire at the feed store. Luckily, no one was hurt.

With a fresh cup of coffee, Cora sat at her desk going over files. Hopefully Virgil would stop by later and she'd see for herself that he was okay.

As she set her cup down, then removed her coat she noticed a letter on her desk. It must've come yesterday because it was too early for today's mail. She picked it up and recognized her mother's handwriting.

A sense of dread overwhelmed her and the palms of her hands grew damp. What did she want? Holding the letter, Cora thought of all the time she was in prison and would've given anything to hold a letter from a family member.

One never came.

Unable to read the letter after all her mother had put her through, Cora placed it on the side of her desk and tried to ignore the plain, white envelope.

Having served in prison for five years, Cora knew what her mother would face. The horror, the pain, the unbearable torment. And while the state had promised reform, she didn't believe it would happen. There might be a slight show of compassion for the public to see, but behind those brick walls was another story all together.

She made her rounds and spoke briefly with Stan. They were expected in surgery this afternoon and she had to prepare. The operation was basically routine, but in her line of business few things went as planned.

Back in her office the letter taunted her, pulling at her natural curiosity. Finally, she picked it up and stared at the beautiful scrawl. Her mother seemed to do everything perfectly, even handwriting.

A tap sounded then Virgil stepped in and closed the door. He smiled, leaned over and kissed her on the lips. His bloodshot eyes spoke of how tired he must be.

"Did you eat breakfast?"

"Yes, thank you for that, I was starving."

"How did it go last night?"

"We don't know anything yet. The explosion scattered the evidence. We have so little to go on, I'm not sure we'll ever get to the bottom of this one."

"You can't connect the two fires?"

"No, there's not enough evidence. I do think the same person is the culprit, but I don't have a clue about who might be guilty."

She leaned back in her chair and studied his handsome face. "You should go home and rest." She scowled at his hands. "You took off your bandages, too. Those blisters are still tender."

"I can't. Ethan and I are talking to all the businesspeople in town to make sure they keep their places locked and secure. Also, we've told the citizens to be on the watch for anything suspicious." Wiggling his fingers, he said, "As for my hands they were filthy. I figured I could find a pretty doctor who could help me with that."

"Hum, flatterer. I can rewrap them before you leave." Looking into his tired face, she wished he would go home after the terrible night he'd had and get some rest. "They really don't know what to look for."

"Anything out of the usual."

Cora shook her head. "I don't know who would do this. Patricia is being released today. She's done very well while here and is anxious to go home."

"She has no home," Virgil said, scrubbing his hands over his face. "There's no place to go."

"I guess they'll stay with her sister for a while until Leonard can reopen his shop."

"Good luck with that. I hope he manages to get back on his feet. There's so much that needs to be done. The town deserves a barber and Leonard is an all right fella."

Taking a deep breath, she held up the letter. "This was on my desk this morning."

"Who's it from?"

"My mother." Cora waved the letter in the air. "What I wouldn't have given for something like this when I was in jail."

"Are you going to read it?"

"I don't know. I can't bring myself to open it. I don't want to get drawn back into that world."

Virgil placed his hat on his bent knee. "They sentence her soon. I'm sure she's frightened."

Cora nodded. "I can imagine but, Virgil, there's nothing I can do for her. The judge isn't going to listen to me." Cora propped her folded arms on her desk. "Especially when she shot Judge Martin in front of a dozen witnesses."

"She's already been found guilty of murder. Now they'll decide if she gets life or death."

"I don't think the judge in St. Louis will sentence her to death. In all honesty, I think they're glad someone got rid of the monster."

Virgil stood. "I don't know what to tell you. If you feel you need to be there, I'll understand."

Her eyes widened and her heart sped up. "Go there?"

"She's still your mother."

"I know, but I can't. God forgive me, I don't think I can."

"Your decision, sweetheart. Whatever you decide, I'll support." He held out his hand. "Do you want to give the letter to me so I can destroy it or are you going to think about it for a while?"

"I need to think."

"All right, I'll see you at home tonight."

"Let's take care of your hands first. Hopefully there won't be another fire."

"Let's keep our fingers crossed."

Cora walked home later that day. She'd put a ham in to cook and needed to prepare the side dishes. Also, she wanted to bake something. For some reason, the busier her hands were the calmer her mind stayed.

With her gloved fists in the pocket of her coat, she fingered the letter from her mother. She'd not yet found the courage to open and read what was inside. It could be horrible and a letter blaming her for everything, or it could be a plea for help. She couldn't imagine her mother begging for anything.

Then again, how often does one face death? Could she let her mother go through that alone? What kind of person, much less a daughter, would do that?

Arriving home, she put her purse down and hurried to Maggie's to collect Jack. He was never happy to leave his friend.

"What did Virgil say about the feed store blowing up?" Maggie asked. "They have any idea who did it?"

"No, and today when he dropped by for a quick visit, I could see the frustration in his eyes. The fear that whoever is doing this could strike again had him pretty edgy."

"Lord, I feel horrible. The church is helping Leonard and Patricia with some clothes and food."

"She was released from the hospital today, so I'm taking a dish to her sister's house tonight."

Maggie nibbled her bottom lip. "I'll prepare something for her tomorrow night. They have to be devastated."

"Understandable."

Cora gathered Jack and headed for the door. "What are you cooking for dinner tonight?"

"I'm not sure yet, but I'll come up with something."

"I baked a big ham. Can Tommy come over and get you some? There's more than enough for two families."

"I appreciate that." She looked at Tommy. "Get your coat on and go with Jack and Aunt Cora."

As Tommy dug in the closet for his coat, Cora took the letter out of her pocket and showed it to Maggie.

Holding it in her hands, her friend gave her a puzzled look. "What's this?"

"A letter from my mother."

Maggie's face paled. "It's not open."

"I can't gather the courage to see what she has to say."

Maggie met her gaze. "Does Virgil know?"

"Yes, and he's okay with whatever I decide."

"Decide what?"

"She's being sentenced soon and I'm thinking the letter is about that."

"But there's nothing you can do."

"I know, but something deep inside me says I should be by her side."

Maggie handed her the letter. "She never stood by you."

"I know. That's what makes this decision difficult."

Maggie put her arm around Cora's shoulders and walked her to the door. "You are no longer involved with that situation in St. Louis. I think it's best if you stay away. You're happy and your mother will only make you feel bad."

"You're right, of course. I just feel so sorry for her."

Maggie put her hands on her hips. "Where was her compassion for her daughter when you were suffering in prison?"

"I know, but I'm stronger."

"That didn't make the suffering any easier."

"I'll send Tommy back with the ham. See you later."

Virgil came in just as she took out the sweet potatoes and rolls from the oven. The cherry pie would have to bake a little longer.

From the doorway he called, "Something smells delicious. I'm starving."

She turned to the sound of his voice. "You're always starved."

He strode to her and pulled her in his arms. After kissing her on the lips, he hugged her tightly against his chest. "This feels better than anything could ever taste."

With her cheek against his beating heart, she closed her eyes and rubbed his back. "I know. Sometimes I wish we were in another world where there was just the three of us."

"You'd miss out on a lot."

"I'd have the people I love and that's all I want."

Jack walked in and looked up at them. "Are you two going to be all mushy or are we gonna eat?"

Cora stepped back. "Sorry, Your Highness."

Jack laughed and Pal barked. "Well, make it snappy."

She glared down at him. "You watch your tone."

Virgil took Jack's hand and led him to the living room. "Guess who he picked that up from?"

Just then, Earl knocked on the back door then entered. Seeing the table not set, he went about taking the dishes out of the cupboard.

"What's going on with the fire at the feed store?" Earl called out to Virgil, who was on his way back to the kitchen. "You find out who did it?"

Helping Cora put the food on the table and slicing the ham, he picked up the coffee pot and looked at Earl. "Not a single idea."

Earl's bushy brows furrowed. "I don't understand all this mess. Why burn down a business? What does that person plan to gain?"

"We don't know."

"Is Dawson helping out?"

"He is and he's very knowledgeable, but when something is blown up, there isn't much left to investigate."

They all sat at the table, Jack said grace and everyone began passing food around. Silence echoed through the small house for a while, but soon, the conversation was back to the fires.

Earl forked a bite of ham. "I contacted a few people in Joplin who have agreed to help out the Caseys until they get on their feet. I saw him and several other men out there cleaning up the mess."

"He wants to get his shop back up and running as soon as possible. That's their only source of income."

"He got a little money from the insurance company," Earl said. "But not near enough because the fire is suspicious."

"It's a shame," Cora said. "I worry that someone might get killed if this continues."

"I don't know what we can do," Earl said, taking a sip of coffee. "Virgil, do you think we should get a committee of volunteers together to walk the streets at night?"

"I don't know about that, Earl. The fire at Leonard's was started in the middle of the day. The feed store was at night, but we don't know when or if the next one will happen."

"Well, we have to make people aware. I hate the thought that a person we know would do something this bad. But a stranger would stand out."

"I spoke to the newspaper and they're running a large ad warning people to be careful and observant."

Cora got up to remove the pie from the oven. "I just hope it doesn't happen again."

Earl pushed his chair back, eyeing the pastry. "That's not likely. There's a reason for this and until we find out why, it's going to keep happening."

Virgil poured more coffee. "I'm wondering if this is a distraction to throw us off something else."

Cora scooped out the cherry pie because there was no way Earl would wait. Jack usually preferred his dessert before bed so he could listen to his program on the radio. "How so, Virgil?"

"This is consuming all my time and resources. We're practically working around the clock and I can't help but worry that someone is diverting our attention while something else is going on."

Earl looked up from his bowl of crumbled cherry pie. "Like what?"

"Well, I thought about the bank. What if someone thinks that robbing the bank while we're chasing our tails is a good idea?"

Earl thought for a moment then said, "Have you talked with Briggs?"

"Yes, and he's hired a retired policeman from Joplin to man the bank until this is solved."

Cora let out a tired breath. "That's good news. I'd hate for anything like a bank robbery to happen."

"I have a few other ideas, too."

Earl smiled. "You really have your brain cooking, don't you?"

"I'm covering all the possibilities."

"You're a smart man, Virgil." Earl picked up his cup. "I don't like you much, but Missy and Jack do, so I'll put up with you."

"Just so you know, Earl. I'm not crazy about you either."

Cora smiled. "You two would give your lives for each other."

Earl shook his head. "Don't count on it." He took the watch from his pocket, flipped it open and checked the time. "Well, I better get home. I need my beauty rest."

"You know, you could sleep for a month and you wouldn't be any prettier," Virgil said with a chuckle.

"I don't know what on God's earth Missy sees in you."

Earl left and Virgil smiled at her. "I don't know either, but I hope you keep seeing it."

She leaned over and kissed him. "I'll always love you."

"What about your mother's letter?" he said, pouring more coffee. "You read it yet?"

"No, but I plan to as soon as Jack goes to bed. You and I will read it together."

"I hope it doesn't upset you. Life is finally getting back to normal now. After that trial in St. Louis, you don't need to invite more trouble."

She bowed her head. "I know, but she's family.

CHAPTER EIGHT

Virgil wished to hell Cora's family would leave her alone. Between her two parents, it was a wonder she wasn't suicidal. Her father was sentenced to life in prison. According to the information Batcher got back to him, Robert Williams took it better than expected.

He'd had great lawyers, fake witnesses, and more excuses than raindrops in a storm but, in the end, the jury found him guilty and sent him off to prison. Thankfully, Cora hadn't heard from him since St. Louis.

Her mother was a different story. The only way to describe Clare Williams was cold, manipulating and heartless. As much as he hated to even think of the possibility, he wouldn't put it past her to do everything possible to ruin Cora's happiness. Virgil suspected she was jealous of her older daughter and had a strange way of showing it.

Jack gobbled down his dessert and tried to stay awake for his favorite radio show. Virgil finally picked up the worn out little boy and tucked him into bed. Pal burrowed as close to Jack as possible. The dog slept right next to the boy every night. He often wondered why Cora hadn't stuck to her guns about the dog sleeping on the back porch, but Jack and Pal were so close, he wasn't going to push the issue.

Cora came in with two small glasses of whiskey from her illegal stash. "We're back to the booze again?"

"I might need it while I read the letter."

After taking a sip, he released a tight breath. The last few days had been grueling and he needed to relax a little. Even now he worried something might happen tonight. His day had started early and every bone in his body ached. But he had to help Cora deal with her mother at the moment. Besides, Ethan was on patrol. The town was in good hands.

Cora placed the letter in her lap and took a sip of whiskey. She looked up at him. "Will you open it?"

"Sure." He took the envelope, slipped his finger beneath the flap and opened the top. He pulled out the letter and handed it to her. "You read it."

He noticed her hands shaking and how pale she'd become. This wasn't easy for her and he resented her mother intruding into their happiness.

Cora unfolded the letter and read it quickly. Then she put it in her lap and took a large gulp of her drink. "She's actually apologizing."

"That doesn't surprise me," he said. "She's going to prison and hoping you'll treat her better than she treated you."

"I guess you're right."

He picked up the two pages of expertly written words. She'd had to have said more than that. "Mind if I read it?"

Cora shook her head, deep in thought.

Clare Williams should've been a damn poet. Her writing was powerful and articulate. An expert at deceit, she preyed on every emotion Cora had. She was graceful, elegant and thoughtful. But, little else. Not one line stated what she felt about her daughter. Nothing that said she loved Cora or even regretted what she'd endured.

No, it was all about Clare.

That and suggesting Cora go to St. Louis for the sentencing because that's the least a good daughter would do for her ailing mother.

"She's not sick, is she?"

After draining her glass, Cora said, "I doubt that very seriously. I could find out easily enough. But, I think she's just grasping at straws."

Studying her closely, Virgil asked, "Are you going?"

"I don't know."

"If you go, her lawyers will ask you to appeal to the jury to be lenient."

"I don't know if I can do that. But, in one way I don't want her to suffer."

He stared at her. "She murdered a man."

"A man worthy of being gunned down." She turned to him, her face bright with anger. "Have you forgotten that Judge Martin killed my sister in cold blood?"

"I can never forget that and neither can you."

Fidgeting, Cora jumped up and began pacing. Her slender fingers twisted together as she agonized over her mother's request. Virgil knew she wanted to do the right thing, but she was also well-schooled in protecting her heart.

The phone rang and they looked at each other. Apprehension clouded the room. Not another fire.

Lunging out of his seat, Virgil reached the phone before the second ring. "Hello."

"It's Ethan, the arsonist has hit again."

Rubbing his face, Virgil hung up and grabbed his coat. "The dry cleaners has been hit. I'll be back as soon as I can."

She ran to kiss him goodbye. Holding her close he inhaled her familiar scent. He had to put a stop to the fires. Life couldn't go on like this. He hadn't slept in hours and he doubted Ethan or Frank had either.

When Virgil arrived, his deputy and the Fire Chief were manning the fire hose to good effect. The fire was well under control. Arthur drove up and hurried toward Virgil. "What's going on?"

"I think someone tried to burn down your business."

"Well, I'll be damned. This is getting ridiculous. How are we supposed to put up with this?"

Carrying an ax slung over his shoulder, Ethan approached. "I got here pretty quick. There isn't a lot of damage. You should be able to make repairs quickly and open back up for business soon."

Virgil handed him a cloth to wipe his face. "Did you see anything?"

"Yeah, a guy about average height and weight ran from behind the store and darted between the grocery store and the tailor shop. I gave chase, but I had to get back to radio in the fire."

Patting his deputy on the back, Virgil said, "I'm thankful you were on your toes or this building and the adjacent ones would've gone up in smoke."

"Frank got here right away and we got the hoses going. Since it was in the back, we managed to contain it before it spread."

Arthur stepped closer. "We'll still have to dry clean everything all over again to get rid of the smell."

Virgil stepped into the middle of the damage. "At least you won't be paying to replace everything."

"I'm worried," Arthur said. "Helen was going to stay late to do payroll. I told her not to bother. She planned to come back after supper. I'm glad I insisted she stay home. If not, she would've been here alone."

Virgil shoved back his hat. "That could've been a disaster."

"You're telling me." Arthur looked at Virgil. "Put a stop to this before the whole city burns down."

"I'm working on it, Arthur. Ethan and I are doing our best. But, now I'm thinking we need people walking the streets at all hours."

His face black with soot, Ethan moved closer. "But we're still back to the fact that the barbershop was set on fire in the middle of the day."

"We'll get more people watching," Virgil said. "Arthur, the business owners in Gibbs City might consider hiring some private security guards from Joplin to stand watch. Briggs has for the bank."

"A lot of smaller businesses can't afford that. So, I want this person caught."

"We'll do our best. Nobody wants him as bad as I do."

Ethan and Virgil got in the squad car and headed back to the office. Inside, Ethan put on a pot of coffee and Virgil slumped down into one of the chairs in the outer office. "Tell me again what the man looked like."

"The one running away?"

"Yeah."

"Well, he was young."

"You saw his face?"

"Didn't have to. He shot out of that shop like a cannon. And when I was close to him, he wasn't even panting."

"A man our age would find that hard to do."

"That's what I figured." Ethan poured a cup of coffee. "Also, when I was chasing him, I heard him laugh."

"What?"

"He laughed like this was a big joke."

"That doesn't sound like a grown man. So, we're looking for an average sized young man. Probably under twenty or twenty-five."

"I'd say that's about right."

"What was he wearing?"

Ethan paced the floor. "I don't know because it was pitch- black."

Virgil poured a cup. "Think, Ethan. Half the stuff we did in the war was at night and neither of us had a problem finding Germans."

"You're right, but this really puzzles me."

"How?"

"Why would a younger person want to hurt the businesses around here?"

"I don't know, but we have to catch the guy."

"Let's think of the younger men in town. There's Archie, Carl's son."

Virgil's back stiffened. "He's not the only one."

"No, I'm saying it wasn't him because this person was thicker. Archie is skin and bones. This guy was used to regular meals."

"There's Sam's boy, Joseph."

"I can't say for sure, but I've never seen Joseph do anything in a hurry."

"What about the Cox's boys?"

"Naw, the oldest would be the only suspect and he's tall. Taller than me."

"Yeah, he takes after his father, Briggs."

"There's the Hamilton boy."

"He's such a mama's boy I doubt he'd do anything without his mother's permission."

"Who does that leave? High School boys?"

"I don't know, but we'll find out what's going on."

Virgil went home to find Cora sleeping and Jack still snuggled in his bed. He let Pal out briefly then when the dog was settled back on the rug next to Jack, Virgil crawled into bed and pulled Cora tightly against him.

She mumbled. "You okay?"

"I'm fine. Sorry I woke you."

"I was going to wait up for you, but I have an early surgery."

He pressed her head to his shoulder. "Go back to sleep. I'll see you in the morning."

She twined her leg over his bare knees. "I think I'm going to St. Louis."

That's not what he wanted her to say. With the fires, he couldn't leave the area and he hated her going alone. "I won't be able to go with you."

"I'm a big girl."

"Yeah, but you're my big girl."

"Don't worry, I'll only stay for the hearing."

The next morning, Virgil wanted to talk to Cora about her decision to attend her mother's sentencing, but when she left for work he was barely awake. He still felt exhausted and he'd fallen into a disturbed sleep. Nightmares of the explosion and his dead comrades kept flashing through his mind. Holding Cora had soothed him as nothing else could.

The day being Friday and her mother's hearing on Monday, Cora would probably leave Sunday. He hated her to go through that for such an ungrateful person, but he didn't want to stand between a mother and daughter.

Thanksgiving was next week. He hoped to have a break in his case by then and Cora back home and in a better frame of mind. That didn't seem to happen very often around there.

He woke Jack up, prodded him to get dressed and finish his cereal. He had insisted both Tommy and Jack ride to school with him instead of walking in the freezing cold. Since the war, Virgil hated the cold. Hated it with a passion.

After dropping the boys off, he made his way to the office. On the way he stopped at Buford and Carl's gas station, Gibbs City Pit Stop. Not needing fuel, he parked and ran inside. "Damn, it's cold out there."

Carl wiped his hands. "I know, and it's made us busier than a hive of bees. Buford and I barely have time to grab a quick bite for lunch."

"That's wonderful."

Buford stuck his head out from under the hood of a Ford. "Don't know what we'd do if your mama didn't run the register for us part-time."

"Yeah, and Archie's been helping out a lot, too."

"Where is he?"

Carl gave him a hard look. "Archie?"

Virgil held out his hands. "I just have a couple of questions for him. He might be able to help us with the fires. And before you go flying off at the mouth, we already know it's not him."

"He's around back, fixing a tire."

Virgil left the garage, stepped through the small store and into the garage bay where flat tires were fixed. "Hey Archie, you got a minute."

"Sure, Sheriff. What you need?"

"Let's step inside. I'm freezing out here."

Once inside, Archie moved over to the wood burning stove and held his hands out to the heat. "I don't like winter any more than you do." He nodded toward the back door. "And the wind whips right through that little area out there."

"You don't have to tell me that. I spent many hours doing exactly what you're doing. Don't forget, my dad owned this filling station first."

"That's right, I almost forgot."

"I assume you've heard about the fires."

Archie looked at him. "Honestly, I could never do nothing like that. When I see how hard my daddy and Buford work, I've gained a much better respect for a business owner."

"We don't suspect you, but do you know any fellas about your age that might?"

Archie looked down at the concrete floor. "No, not really. I'm pretty sure my friends wouldn't. I heard Mrs. Casey went to the hospital?"

"That's right."

Archie shook his head. "That's too scary."

"Nobody comes to mind, huh?"

Archie looked out the window. "Not unless you look across the street."

Virgil joined Archie and stared at the empty bays for Eddie and Son's Gas Station. "He has two older boys."

"Yeah, and they ain't happy we're open for business."

"His oldest is about twenty isn't he?"

"I don't know, but I keep a sharp eye out on them. I'm afraid they'll do something to run us off."

Virgil left Archie and went back out to see Carl. "Listen, it just came to my attention that Eddie and Son's aren't doing so well. Stay sharp."

"Me and Buford are taking turns at night with a loaded shotgun and leaving the lights on. We ain't taking any chances."

"Good idea."

Virgil didn't want to leave Carl's gas station and drive directly to Eddie's but he would be talking to the man before the day was over.

CHAPTER NINE

Cora left surgery feeling good about her patient. Miss Mulberry had survived a very delicate heart surgery and it would be touch and go for a few days.

Rolling her tense shoulders, she headed to the nurse's station for a cup of coffee. While there, one of the aides asked her if she was enjoying married life. Cora couldn't be happier and, while nothing could ruin that happiness, her mother's letter had cast a shadow on her thoughts.

In her office, she re-read the letter again, and found it impatient and cold. Her mother showed no change of heart or a desire to make amendments. Cora wondered if her mother's lawyer had put her mother up to asking her to attend the hearing in the hopes of gaining the judge's sympathy. Most of the letter was filled with complaints and inconveniences she suffered. The pride that coursed through her Southern veins hadn't been diluted by current events.

Even knowing she could be sent to the electric chair didn't seem to bother her as much as the discomfort of living in a cell. Cora knew the smart thing to do would be to ignore everything and go on with her life. She was happy for once, why couldn't she leave well enough alone?

It's not like her mother begged her on bended knees to come to her defense and be a character witness. No, she'd simply complained about the rough blanket, lack of privacy and the food.

She had no idea what she was in for. Prison was a hundred times worse than jail. If only she could make her understand that. Prepare her to be tougher and stronger, but her mother's strength lay elsewhere. Her proper upbringing and extravagant lifestyle had her spoiled, but also made her cunning enough to survive the strongest battles.

Still, prison chewed up and spit out women like Clare Williams every day of the week. They'd break her spirit no matter how stubborn she was. There would be little left when the authorities were through with her.

In her heart, even as unloving as her mother had been to her, Cora wanted to spare her mother that kind of pain. But, at the same time, she was very familiar with the way Clare manipulated people, especially her.

Virgil stepped into her office with a bag of hamburgers and fries from Betty's Diner. "It's better than hospital food."

Cora smiled. "I agree. And I'm very happy to see you."

"I thought you would be. I've been so busy lately, I've hardly been home."

"Let's do something Saturday."

While her mouth watered, he unwrapped his burger. "You leaving for St. Louis Sunday?"

She lowered her head. He didn't want her to go. "I think so."

"The roads are a mess."

"Let's hope the bus driver is careful."

"Will you come home as soon as you can?"

She placed her hand on his wrist, just above the red marks from the burns, and squeezed. "I won't stay a minute longer than I have to."

"Good, Jack and I are only good so long without your cooking." He lowered his head and leaned closer. "Earl isn't going to be pleased, either."

She laughed. "I know that's the only reason you two keep me around."

Virgil sent her a sexy grin. "I'm not speaking for Jack, but while your cooking is good, there are other things about you I like better." Then he winked, making her cheeks flare with heat.

"You're making me blush."

He shrugged. "We're married adults. You should be over the whole embarrassing stuff." He took a bite of his burger.

"Well, I am in public."

"We're alone."

She narrowed her eyes. "You're flirting with your own wife."

"So, a man's gotta right to if he wants."

She took a sip of her cola and leaned back to enjoy his flattery and the tasty food. "So how's the investigation going?"

"Not a damned thing yet. We can't figure out why this person is setting fire to places."

"Are they robbing them first, maybe?"

"I thought that could be the problem, but Newman said his cash register was full of money and when we found it, the cash was still in it."

"And there wasn't any money to be gained at the barbershop."

"The dry cleaners always puts their cash in a safe. There's no reason to rob that place unless you can break the combination, and most crooks can't."

"None of it makes any sense at all."

Virgil took a drink of his cola. "I'm afraid someone is going to end up dead in one of these fires."

"Oh dear, that's a horrible thought."

"I'm sorry to say, but after dinner tonight I'm on the streets and you might check with Miss Winters to watch Jack this weekend because I'll be out there until this person is caught."

"I'll call her this evening. Earl's not going to like her being there."

"Earl doesn't like anything but you and Jack."

"He likes you too."

"Humph. I wouldn't count on it."

After eating, she checked his hands and gave him some salve for the burns. Virgil refused to wear bandages any longer. After a quick kiss, he left and Cora went back to work. In her office, she called her mother's attorney in St. Louis to inform him she'd be at the hearing and asked if there was anything she could do to help.

The man didn't sound very reassuring. He thought her mother stood a very good chance of being executed because the Martin family had been so verbal and many of Judge Martin's sketchy friends were laying it on pretty thick.

Cora didn't care about that. Her mother had killed a violent, dangerous man. They should be giving her a medal for bravery because she did what the authorities hadn't been able to do for years. One single shot had ended Judge Martin's reign of terror.

Leaving work, Cora headed to JJ's office. He was always the voice of reason in these situations. She had to wait several minutes before JJ could see her, but once the door closed, he pulled her into a friendly embrace.

She said, "I've missed you."

"I've missed you too, but we both have such important jobs," JJ said. Then they both broke out laughing.

Cora smiled and took a seat. "Listen to us. You'd think we were somebody."

"I know, every time I walk into the office, I think, am I really the Assistant District Attorney?"

"They're lucky to have you and your brilliant mind."

"Ha."

"I bet your father is very proud of you. I know Aunt Rose would be."

JJ stuck his hands in his pocket and stared out the small window that faced the courthouse. "I wish things had been different for them. If only the world was more understanding."

"Someday it will be. But, I have no doubt in my mind that Aunt Rose loved you and your father. She was a good woman."

"The best," JJ said. "I'm glad I got to know her."

"I'm glad I got to know you."

He laughed and leaned against his desk and crossed his arms. "I know you well enough to know that you don't come to my office unless you have a question. So what is it?"

She handed him her mother's letter and sat back while he read it.

Tossing the pages on his desk, he looked at her. "Don't tear yourself apart trying to save her. She didn't lift a finger for you when you were suffering."

"I know, but I like to think I'm a better person than she is."

JJ rubbed his chin. "And that's exactly what Clare Williams is counting on. She deliberately led your father to think you belonged to another man. What kind of mother does that?"

Cora shook her head. "I can't defend her, JJ. I don't believe anyone can. But she's still my mother."

His eyes softened. "I can understand. It's difficult to try to have a relationship with our parents. They have no idea the impact they have on our lives."

Cora looked at her folded hands. "I love her no matter what she's done."

"What about your father?"

"No, I can't forgive him. He was a monster my whole life."

"He didn't know you were his child."

"Should I suffer for that? I was only a child used as a pawn by two very devious people."

"And your mother sat back and watched the whole thing. She never came to your aid, cleared the air with your father, or even pretended to care."

Cora stood. "Everything you say is true, but I have to see her. If she's sent to the electric chair this will be the last time I see her."

"Are you stopping by the prison to visit your father?"

"No, I won't give him the satisfaction. They've never been fair to me. And he of all people isn't worthy of my time."

JJ stood and walked her to the door. "I wish I could go with you, but I'm tied up."

She touched his arm. "I'll be fine. I won't be but a day or two."

He pulled her closer for a hug and a peck on the cheek. "Be careful."

She left JJ's office and hurried home. Virgil would be worried about where she had been. The man was so protective concerning her. While she loved him deeply for being the first man in her life that ever showed her such devotion, she knew he wasn't going to be happy.

At home, Virgil and Jack were playing with Pal, who ran in circles barking. He smiled up at her. "I didn't start supper because I wasn't sure what you had planned."

Jack knelt next to Pal. "I wanted him to fix hot dogs, but he said you didn't like them."

"They're okay, but I don't want them for supper. Tonight, it's leftovers. I know you two are starving as usual, so I'll get busy."

She put her purse on the table next to the couch and tied on her apron as she moved toward the stove.

Virgil came in. "Still determined to go to St. Louis?"

She avoided his gaze. "Yes, I spoke to JJ and he isn't any happier about the situation than you are."

"Maybe because we're both making sense."

She turned and wrapped her arms around his neck and kissed him on the lips. A spark of passion seared through her body and she wished it was bedtime. "The two of you love me very much and want to protect me from any harm that might come my way. But this is something I have to do."

"I understand. I don't like it." He tapped her on the nose. "But I know the kind of woman you are."

"I'd better hurry and get supper on the table before you and Jack die of starvation."

They chuckled, then Virgil took the dishes out of the cupboard. Jack read aloud from his school book until the food was placed on the table. "Go wash up, Jack," Virgil said. "Supper's ready."

Right on time, Earl came in the back door and looked at the dishes on the table. "Leftovers?"

"That's right," Virgil said. "But there's Betty's Diner if you don't like it."

"Don't be so damned snappy, young fella. I ain't complaining. I'm admiring the fact that Missy can make anything taste good."

"Take a seat, Earl. Coffee will be ready soon."

Virgil passed the dish of potatoes around. "You know Cora is leaving for St. Louis Sunday?"

Cora shot her husband a dark look. She knew Virgil was sly enough to try and pull her neighbor into the discussion. No doubt Earl would have an opinion and most likely it would be the same as her husband's.

CHAPTER TEN

Virgil knew he wasn't playing fair, but he'd do about anything in his power to keep Cora from going to St. Louis. Fear she'd get there and be hurt and rejected again made his insides nervous. How much could the poor woman take?

If it weren't against the law, he'd strangle Clare Williams for sending Cora that letter. He knew what she was up to and, God, he hated that her little scheme had worked. The daughter that she'd shunned all her life would try to rescue her from what she rightfully deserved.

"Whatcha going there for?"

"I received a letter from my mother. Her sentencing hearing is Monday."

Earl stabbed a pork chop with his folk. "What's that got to do with you?"

Keeping his head down, Virgil spoke up. "She wants to testify so the judge won't execute Clare."

Cora put her fork down and dabbed her lips. "That's not exactly the truth, Virgil, and you know it. I simply want to be there in hopes that the judge will be more lenient if there is a family member there, that's all."

"Sounds like the same thing to me," Earl said. "Let her rot. She was never a mother to you and didn't lift a finger to help you when they threw you behind bars. That woman didn't show an ounce of compassion."

"What's compassion?" Jack asked.

"It means love or concern for another person."

"You mean your mama didn't like you?"

Virgil had forgotten Jack was listening to everything. "No, son, she isn't a very nice lady. She said some mean things that hurt your Aunt Cora."

"Please Virgil, she didn't really..."

"Don't go," Jack said. "If someone isn't nice to you, you don't have to be nice to them."

Earl buttered a slice of bread. "The boy makes more sense than you going to St. Louis."

Obviously upset, Cora stood, shoving back her chair. "I'm going because the woman gave birth to me and I know what it feels like to be abandoned. And while she wasn't decent to me, in my heart, I have compassion."

"It's a waste of time," Earl snapped. "She wouldn't throw a glass of water on you if you were on fire."

"That's probably true. But, I'm going." She looked at Jack. "Sometimes those who treat you the worst deserve your best."

Cora left the room and Virgil took a sip of coffee. "Well, that didn't fly."

"You're her husband. Tell her not to go. It's as simple as that."

"You think I'm the kind of man who'd do something like that to his wife? She'd never tolerate that and I won't make demands on her."

Jack stuffed a spoonful of corn in his mouth. "Well, you tell me I can't go places all the time."

"That's because I want you safe."

"Don't you want Aunt Cora safe?"

"Yes, I do. More than anything in the world, but she's grown up and I can't boss her around."

A sober grunt escaped from Earl's mouth. "The hell you can't. Her going up there is going to rip her heart out."

Everything Earl said was true and Virgil hated when Cora hurt, but he could only protect her heart so much. She had to go for her own good. Would she be crushed? Probably, but this wasn't his call.

"I agree."

Rising slowly, Earl stood up and brought the coffee pot to the table. "You not going with her?"

"I have a crazy person trying to burn the town down. I need to be here."

Topping off Virgil's coffee, Earl returned the pot to the stove. "Well, I'm going then."

"You can't make a trip like that in this weather. I'm worried enough about Cora."

Eyes squinted, Earl pointed a finger at Virgil. "I'm going and you ain't got nothing to say about it."

"I can say all I want. She's my wife."

"Well, I ain't allowing her to go there by herself. God only knows what can happen."

"She may not want you to go."

"I don't give a rat's ass. I'll go if I want to and she can just take it or leave it."

Earl set his coffee mug down with a thump, stood and pulled on his coat as he walked out the door, leaving Virgil concerned. Their neighbor wasn't a young chicken anymore and he'd hate for him to overdo it and get sick. But, in his heart, he was glad Cora would have someone to lean on.

The next morning at breakfast, after Jack had left for school, he offered to take Cora to work. "Have you bought your bus ticket yet?"

"No, I need to do that," she said, sipping her second cup of coffee. "Maybe I can do it later today."

"I'll take care of that. Earl has offered to accompany you."

Her eyes shot up and she pinned his with an irritated glare. "You shouldn't have done that. Earl isn't that healthy and needs to stay home where he belongs."

"I didn't put him up to it. He made up his own mind. If you can change it, more power to you. But you know how stubborn he can be."

"I do, but I'm going to try to talk some sense into his hard head."

Virgil stood, leaned over for a quick kiss and headed for the door. "Good luck changing his mind."

He arrived at his office to find Ethan half-asleep with his head down on the desk. The deputy raised his gaze and blinked. "Howdy, Sheriff. We had a quiet night." He arched his back and stretched.

"Good, you go home and get some rest."

"Much obliged. I'm exhausted."

Ethan didn't stay to talk and Virgil didn't blame him. No doubt he'd been out patrolling all night without any breaks and that was rough on a body no matter your age.

Yawning, he moved the percolator to the heated plate on the stove and waited for it to warm up. As soon as he could break away, he'd go to the bus station and get Cora's ticket. Sleeping on it hadn't changed his mind. He still wished she would stay home and let Clare deal with her own mess.

As he poured the hot brew into a cup, the judge came in. "Morning, Virgil."

"Judge. What brings you here?" He took a sip of the mud left over from last night and crunched up his face. "I know it's not the coffee."

"No, but I heard Cora is going to St. Louis."

Virgil straightened. "News sure travels fast in this little town."

"I don't think that's a wise move. Odds are the judge has already made up his mind."

"I'm sure you're right, but I can't stop her. She wants to be there for her mother."

"I can't imagine why. Clare Williams was never there for her."

"Compassion."

"That doesn't mean much in a court of law. I'm thinking Clare will spend the rest of her life in prison."

"Not the electric chair?"

The judge placed his hat the corner of the chair Ethan had left then leaned his hips on the side of the desk. "I don't think any man likes to sentence a woman to the electric chair. At least, until now."

"I don't think that will happen either."

Pacing angrily, the judge said, "That's why Cora going there is a waste of time. Her mother committed cold-blooded murder regardless of who she shot. There was a courtroom full of people who saw her shoot Judge Martin, so it comes down to doing the right thing."

"I'm sure Cora will suffer if she goes."

Folding his arms, Garner stared at him. "I did hear that her father isn't doing too well in prison. I guess all this has been a strain on his heart and he spends more time in sickbay than in his cell."

"That doesn't break my heart one bit. As a matter of fact, I'd love to kick up the process if I could."

"I wish you could talk Cora out of going. It would save her a lot of heartache."

"She's too stubborn."

"Well, the time couldn't be worse with these fires."

"Earl is insisting on going with her."

The judge's brows rose. "Well, let him. He's a damned smart man and he'll protect her."

"He's a nosey old fart."

The judge smiled. "You don't know Earl at all."

"I see way more of him than I like."

"He's crazy about Cora. Use that. Let him go. You won't regret it. He has a lot of connections in St. Louis."

Another mystery about Earl Clevenger. "What is it with that guy. Was he President of the United States once and I didn't hear about it?"

Laughing mysteriously, the judge took his hat and walked out the door, leaving Virgil to worry about Cora being away from him. He settled into his chair and was about to get several piles of paperwork done when Frank burst through his door.

"Fire! The school!"

Virgil's blood turned to ice and his head spun. Jack!

Grabbing his coat and hat, he hit the door running and was in the squad car and racing to the school long before Frank could get the fire truck backed out of the bay.

Siren's screaming, lights flashing, Virgil had the gas pedal pushed practically through the floorboard. When he reached the end of Main and turned onto Nash Street he saw the smoke. Slamming his foot on the brake, he cut the ignition, jumped out and ran toward the children gathered outside, away from the fire.

"Jack, Jack, where are you?"

"I'm here, Uncle Virgil."

Jack and Tommy ran toward him and wrapped their arms around his waist. Miss Potter quickly approached.

"Is every student accounted for?" Virgil asked.

Pete Russell came over wiping his bald head with a white, linen handkerchief. "Yes, we managed to get everyone out."

Frank arrived and he and several men began putting out the fire. Virgil kept the children away from danger. They were curious, but a fire was no place for grade-schoolers.

Miss Potter was visibly shaking. He stepped over to her. "What happened?"

"I was reading when I suddenly smelled smoke. About that time, Mr. Russell came running into my class and shouted for us all to get out."

His eyes traced the heads of all the children. "You're sure no one was left behind?"

"Yes, we all filed very quickly out of the room, down the hall and exited the building. As soon as we were outside, each teacher did a roll call and there wasn't anyone not accounted for."

"Take the children down the block to the church so they'll be out of the cold. Today's the ladies' bible study so it isn't locked. The kids should be safe there until their parents pick them up. Some of their folks are already here. Have Principal

Russell stay behind to let the rest know what's going on." Not waiting for a response, he hurried off to find the Fire Chief.

Virgil walked around the end of the building and found Frank and a few men hosing down the last of the flames. It didn't look like much damage was done, but it could've been a tragedy.

Weary and covered in soot, Frank walked over to him. "What the hell is going on? This fire was set and they even left the damned can right there on the step."

"This is one bold son of a bitch." Virgil looked around at the vacant lot behind the school and several smaller homes. They were the first houses built in the area and many of the residents were elderly. "I'll check over there and see if anyone saw anything."

"I doubt they did. And as far away as the houses are, they probably couldn't tell who was out here."

"I have to ask anyway."

Frank looked at the children trooping behind their teacher toward the church. "This could've been the worst day in our history."

"I know and this has to stop. I can't have someone running around my county who has the nerve and lack of conscience to set the school on fire."

Yanking the door of his squad car open, Virgil slid in and drove through the neighborhood. When he came to the Archer's residence, he knocked and they let him inside. They hadn't seen anything but they let him use their phone to call Cora so she wouldn't worry about Jack.

None of the people he talked to had seen anything. One man said he saw someone walking across the field, but he didn't see a can in his hand. Virgil tried to still his shaking hands without any luck. Damn, he was mad.

Back at the fire, Virgil picked up Jack and Tommy as well as little Ronnie and took them home. When he explained to Susan Welsh what'd happened, she broke down crying. Maggie looked like she was about to collapse. As soon as she had the boys settled in the kitchen eating cookies, she turned back to Virgil, anger in every line on her face. "Get that monster."

Back at his office, he'd barely removed his heavy coat when the interim Mayor, Clark McBride came into his office. For some reason Virgil didn't like the man who had taken the young Curtis Powell's place after he died of influenza.

Older and more set in his ways, Clark sometimes acted like they were still in the stone ages. Hell, he had no idea what progress was except he didn't want anything to do with it.

Shaking his finger and raising his voice, Clark blustered, "Virgil, I want whoever is setting these fires caught. If you're not the man to do it, I'll find someone else."

Disgusted, Virgil turned away. "You don't have that kind of authority and we both know it. I work for the County, not your city. I'm doing all I can. You want to assign me another deputy, I'd really appreciate it. Otherwise, get out of my office."

"Now see here, we've got to work together."

"Not if you think you can come into my office and push me around by making threats, we don't."

Leaning heavily on Virgil's desk, the man appeared shaken. "I apologize for that, but I have parents banging on my door."

"Send them to me. I have no problem telling them I'm doing all I can and could use a little more help."

Frantically walking in circles, Clark confessed. "I don't know what to do." His eyes pleaded. "Maybe I can have private citizens walking the streets."

"People have jobs and this arsonist hits at all hours. Day or night. It's not like there is a pattern I can follow. I have my deputy working at night to keep an eye on the businesses. I have to tell you, I never expected the school to be hit. Not with children inside."

Calmer now, Clark wiped his face and lowered his voice, "You come up with something, please call my office. And I'll get you an extra man if it's my son-in-law. He's working the evening shift at the foundry. He can help patrol the city during the day."

"I have a lot on my plate right now. I'm talking to Judge Garner later today. The last thing I want is a bunch of panicked civilians with guns shooting at anything that moves"

CHAPTER ELEVEN

Cora practically ran all the way home from work. The thought of something happening to Jack had her in a state of utter panic. A fire at the school full of children. What was the world coming to? Scared out of her mind, she ran faster as she neared Maggie's house.

Stumbling up the porch steps, Cora pounded on the door. "Maggie, Maggie is Jack in there?"

Her friend opened the door and enveloped her in a warm hug. "He's fine."

Cora pressed her hand to her chest. "Thank God." Relief washed over her and her heart settled down. "I was so frightened when Virgil called."

"I was shocked when I heard someone had set out to hurt our children." Maggie tightened her lips. "I could kill whoever is doing this."

"I think I could too."

Jack ran toward her and Cora knelt and held out her arms. "Virgil told me you were okay, but I had to see for myself."

"Me and Tommy and Ronnie were not burned up in the fire."

"Were you frightened?"

Tommy joined them, his new clothes nicely pressed. "Naw, we just wanted to see the fire truck."

"Yeah, that's all we were thinking about," Jack said but the stark expression on his face told her that wasn't the case. He'd been frightened. Maybe not then, but he was now.

She took his little, warm hand in hers. "I think Jack and I are going home for the day."

They left and walked across the street. Cora noticed how tightly Jack held on to her. He hadn't wanted to appear frightened in front of Tommy or Ronnie. The incident had rattled him to some degree and that meant she had no intention of returning to work.

Inside, she removed their coats and turned on the radio. She sat on the couch waiting for her nerves to settle down. It didn't take long for Jack to crawl onto her lap, his ears tuned to the sound of the Lone Ranger.

Hiding a smile, she was content that her little boy was safe in her arms. How did a mother survive the death of a child? She couldn't.

Soon, Jack was calm enough for her to contact Doctor Janson and let him know what'd happened and to notify him she wouldn't be returning to work.

She changed clothes and went into the kitchen to find something to bake because that always calmed her nerves and distracted her from the thought of losing someone she loved so much. Jack curled up on the sofa with Pal in his lap. She heard him telling the dog about the fire.

As she put the mincemeat pie in the oven, the front door opened and Virgil came in, his face etched with worry. He'd been afraid for Jack as well. She'd heard it in his voice on the phone. She ran to him and wrapped her arms around his strong body and allowed the security of his embrace to soothe her entire body.

"I was so frightened," she murmured. "If anything ever happened, I'd die."

"I know, I would too. I don't think I've ever driven so fast in my life."

"I'm glad you called me at the hospital because if I'd heard the news from anyone else I would've fallen completely apart."

"I know, I know." He gently cupped the back of her head, holding her tightly. She knew he stared over at Jack on the couch, petting Pal.

Stepping back, she said, "I'm glad it's over."

"It's not over yet. Not until I find the person responsible. He might never make it to jail."

"What kind of person would do that? I hate thinking we live in a place where this could happen."

"I know, I look every citizen in the eyes and I wonder, are you the one?"

"Come in the kitchen, I just put on a pot of coffee."

"That means Earl should be here any moment."

"Virgil, be nice. He's a good man."

As if on cue, the back door opened and Earl burst into the room. "Is Jack okay."

"Everyone is fine, Earl," Virgil said. "The fire was started in the back of the building. The kids had plenty of time to get out."

"What in the hell is happening? This place is going to hell in a handbasket when some lunatic sets fire to a schoolhouse full of children."

Cora set out three cups. "I completely agree."

"Virgil," Earl said, dead serious. "I want whoever is responsible in jail."

Tight-lipped, Virgil glanced at their neighbor. "You think I'm not trying my best?"

"I know you are, but you have to work faster."

"I've already had this argument with the mayor."

Earl slapped the table. "He ain't no mayor. He's a jackass and that's all there is to it."

"Well, the town council appointed him to be in charge until the next election."

"That don't mean he has the right to tell you how to do your job."

"Don't act like you have the right."

Earl stirred his coffee. "I'm different. I'm practically family. He's a blowhard."

Cora took the pie out of the oven to cool. She doubted it would stay there long once Earl saw it. She took down three saucers and pulled out a chair at the table. Virgil was worried, and Earl was mad, but Cora's emotions were in turmoil. Fear for Jack, grateful he was okay, and desperate to protect her child.

"I'm glad to be getting out of town for a couple of days, but now I'm worried about what's going to catch on fire next."

Virgil took a sip of his coffee and ran his fingers through his hair. "I had Ethan on duty all night, prowling the streets looking for anyone up to mischief and nothing happened. Then in broad daylight the arsonist strikes in the most unlikely spot in town."

"I never thought anyone would put the kids at risk."

Earl looked over at Jack still in the living room. "That's a sick person. How on earth could he be so sure something wouldn't go wrong and one of the kids gets hurt? Maybe burned alive."

Cora held out her hand. "Please don't say that, Earl. It's too frightening. I don't want to upset Jack any more than he is already."

"Yeah, we've got enough on our plates." Virgil looked at Earl. "Today I'm checking out all the places a man can buy kerosene. Since that was used at the barbershop and maybe the school, there has to be a supplier."

"You're right. The person buying up a lot of kerosene would draw suspicion."

Cora put the pie on the table. "But it is winter."

"That's right, but still, that's a lot of fuel for the last four days. Someone would notice that."

"Yes, they would," Earl agreed. "Plus, I heard they left the can behind. Those are expensive. Most people don't do that."

"I'm checking the gas stations and the general store."

Cora bit her lip. "They could've shopped in the surrounding towns."

"They could, but most people around here know each other. Someone traveling a distance to buy kerosene would be noticed."

After a heavy sigh, Virgil stood, walked over and hugged the young boy who was dozing off. Slipping on his coat, he looked back at her. "I'll be home for dinner." He pointed to Earl. "Save me a piece of that pie."

"You can have the whole damn thing. I don't like mincemeat."

Virgil stopped, wide eyed. "Really? There's a pie you don't like?"

"That's the only one."

That managed to bring a smile to Cora's face. "I never imagined that for a minute. I'm sorry. I'll bake a peach pie for dinner."

"That's better."

Opening the back door, Earl shouted to Virgil, "Get busy finding that crazy bastard."

Both doors closed.

Cora was tempted to take a little nap this afternoon. She didn't realize how exhausted she was. Perhaps it was her nerves, but her body felt like she'd run a race.

Cleaning the kitchen, she did the dishes, put in a chicken to bake and moved to the couch with Jack. "Can I go to Tommy's and play?"

"I'd like you to stay with me this afternoon. What happened at the school today really frightened me."

Jack crawled into her lap. "I didn't want Tommy to know, but I was really scared until Uncle Virgil showed up. I was afraid we'd all burn up."

She brushed his hair back and smiled. "I'm so thankful that didn't happen." She kissed his cheek. "I'd be so lost without you."

"You know, Aunt Cora, I'd be sad if you went away and I had to go live somewhere else."

"I'll never go away."

"But, what if you die like my mother?"

"I'm going to try to not let that ever happen."

"I hope you live forever."

"So do I." She squeezed him tight. "Don't worry about what might or might not happen. Let's just enjoy what we have." She knew things could change in an instant. But, she worried enough for both of them.

For the longest time, Cora and Jack sat on the couch enjoying the peace of being together and safe. While Cora didn't know everyone in town, she couldn't imagine anyone who'd want to harm the children.

One could say the arsonist had been careful to keep the fire far from where the children were, but a student could've been wandering the halls for all they knew.

Her heart pounded against her ribcage and she struggled to keep her breathing under control. Jack meant everything to her and Virgil. Their lives would be so empty without him there to love. And the horror of knowing he suffered through a fire would simply be the end of her existence. She couldn't live with that.

Knowing Jack would be their only child made him all the more special. While Virgil treated her nephew as his own, Jack was her blood and meant more than her own life.

Cora pressed her hand to her stomach. She would never have her own baby. Three forced abortions had ruined any chance she might have had at becoming a mother. She bit back tears and pressed her lips on the top of Jack's head.

It simply wasn't meant to be.

CHAPTER TWELVE

In the judge's chambers, Virgil slumped in the chair in front of his desk. Judge Garner sat smoking a pipe, his face troubled, his eyes sad. "I heard about the school and it turns my stomach. How can someone put the lives of young children in harm's way like that?"

"I want this son of a bitch so bad I can taste it. When I find whoever did this, don't expect him locked up in jail before I get the chance to stomp him to pieces."

The judge leaned back. "We can't have any of that and you know it. But, his ass will hang, that's for sure."

"Who can you think of that might do something like this?"

"I've been doing nothing but contemplating that very question. I didn't come up with a single person. And there's no logic to all this. The fires are random."

"I agree," Virgil said. "If I saw even a hint of a pattern I'd have something to go on, but this is plain crazy."

"Well, the school was the last straw. I'm calling a town hall meeting and we're going to get some help guarding the city. You and Ethan can't do this alone."

Virgil let out a tired breath. "I just spoke to the mayor and he's of the same mind. Even went as far as to offer up his son-in-law."

The judge's face turned sour. "That no-account bum can't guard a chicken house. He's useless."

"I agree, but we must do something."

"You talk to Gene McKinnon?"

"This isn't federal."

The judge's brow arched. "He's still a good friend and might have a few things to offer."

Virgil didn't understand. "Like what?"

"Manpower."

"We can't have federal agents prowling the streets. That would panic every citizen in the town. I'll check with Gene, but I'm not keen on them coming in here and taking over."

"I agree with you there. I just thought he'd have some ideas."

Virgil came to his feet. "I'm checking around today. I'll see you at the town hall meeting tonight."

Outside in the freezing weather, he drove down Main Street, his eyes searching every inch of the area for anything unusual. All appeared quiet and he hoped it stayed that way.

He pulled into Eddie and Son's Gas Station and killed the engine. Carl and Buford's business had put a pretty good dent into Eddie Summerfield's cash register. There wasn't a customer in sight and not a vehicle in the garage bay to be repaired.

Smiling widely, Eddie came out wiping his hands on a grease rag. Virgil didn't know why because they were already clean as a bank teller's.

"What's going on, Sheriff?"

"Nothing, thought I'd drop by and see if anyone had stopped by here lately buying up a lot of kerosene."

"No, I haven't had that kind of business. Besides, I don't sell much of that."

"But you have it on the property?"

"Sure, we're a gas station. We use it to clean car parts. Once in a while someone will come in and buy a gallon or two, but we've never kept much on hand."

Virgil looked across the street, his eyes landing on Carl and Buford's place of business. "They seem to be really busy."

"Yeah, but I've stashed back enough money to hold out. I think people will turn around soon and we'll be back to normal."

"You losing money?"

"Not as much as you might think. I'm still managing to hang on to my usual customers." He pointed across the street. "I'm losing most of my business because of Buford. He's the best mechanic in the area. Carl too."

"Well, I'll let you go." Virgil got back into the car. "If you notice anything unusual, be sure to let me know."

"We're keeping an eye on things."

"Yeah, blowing up a gas station could possibly cause a lot of damage to the town."

"That's why one of my sons is on duty every night. Nobody's going to burn my business to the ground."

Eddie's confidence spoke volumes to Virgil, but then again, he had three strong, healthy boys to look after the place.

The car wipers kept the newly falling snow from sticking to his windshield as he drove to his folk's house to see how they were doing. As soon as he opened the door, the delicious aroma of pumpkin pie wafted up his nose and made him smile. "That smells delicious."

His mother hugged him and they made their way to the kitchen. "Your daddy was just saying the same thing. While I made those for Thanksgiving, I think we can spare you two men a nice slice with a cup of coffee."

Hanging his hat on the empty chair beside him, Virgil rubbed his hands together. "I'll agree with that." His father's smile spread all the way across his face. "We need to see how good they are." Virgil winked. "Can't have you ruining the holiday."

Minnie Carter fisted her hands on her hips. "Now you listen here. Nobody can bake a better pumpkin pie than I can. So, don't you go getting ornery or I might change my mind about sharing my dessert."

Virgil folded his arms on the table and didn't flinch. No way would he allow his mouth to cheat him out of a piece of his mother's pie. During the war, he used to dream about sitting at this table, eating his mother's best pie.

With two saucers on the table and coffee being poured, Virgil leaned back and looked at his dad. "I can hardly wait to dig in."

Patting him on the shoulder, his mother chuckled. "You never could."

A moment later, he was savoring every bite, not even bothering to wash it down with coffee. No, that would wait until later. Right now, he let the cinnamon, nutmeg, and pumpkin have a party in his mouth.

Shoving the empty plate way, Virgil picked up his cup and took a sip. "That's your best ever."

His mother took a seat beside him and nudged him on the shoulder. "Aw, you always say that."

"Only because it's true," his dad said. "That's why you always used to beat Wanda Clevenger when it came to pumpkin pie."

Minnie smiled. "It was a friendly rivalry. I loved Wanda like a sister. The state fair isn't fun now that there isn't any decent competition."

Virgil leaned back. "I bet Cora could give you a run for your money."

"She that good?" his father asked. "That would be wonderful if she entered the pie baking contest."

"I'll mention it, but Cora isn't one to draw a lot of attention. She's pretty happy right now and I want her to stay that way."

"Good," his mother said. "She's a wonderful person."

"I'm afraid she's in for trouble soon."

His mother looked worried. "Really?"

"Her mother wants Cora to go to St. Louis next week for her sentencing hearing."

"Is she going after all her parents have done to her?"

"She's going, all right. I can't say I agree with her decision, but it's between her and her family."

"I hope they don't drag her into something else."

94

"Earl is going with her, so he'll protect her. With everything going on in town, I can't leave."

"Yes, he's very good about that kind of thing."

His mother stood and went to the sink. His father captured his attention. "What about all these fires?"

"I don't have a clue what's going on. There's no reason for anyone to want to harm the businesses in Gibbs City. No disagreements or bad feelings that we know of. The judge and I have been racking our brains."

His dad looked worried. "I hate to say anything, but I worry about Carl and Buford's business. If that were to be set on fire, the town would suffer a lot of damage."

"I know, I've warned them and they're standing guard around the clock."

"I'm going in later today and make sure that they understand how important that is."

Virgil shoved back his chair. "I'm heading that way, need a lift?"

"Sure, let me get my coat and hat."

As he and his father rolled into town, he noticed Caroline Dixon walking out of the drug store. She waved and smiled. Virgil couldn't figure out for the life of him why she and Ethan didn't get married. They were obviously in love with each other, but both were afraid to make a move.

Virgil chuckled. Since when had he become Cupid?

As he pulled into the gas station Carl and Buford had named Gibbs City Pit Stop, he saw the men were busy at work. Buford came out and shook his hand. "We're so full we can't keep up with the work."

Carl joined them. "We're thinking of hiring another person to take up the slack."

Virgil's father left the car. "We'll talk about that. Maybe I could come in daily and get a few things done."

"That would be great," Carl said. "You know the business better than anyone."

His father's gaze drifted across the street. "How are they taking Carl and Buford's success?"

95

Virgil shrugged. "Eddie says he has enough money for the long haul and a little competition isn't going to run him out of business."

Virgil's dad headed inside. "Wonder where he got that from. He mortgaged his house to get the loan for the gas station to begin with."

Virgil stared across the street. Eddie hadn't seemed worried at all and he was almost pleased that Carl and Buford had started a business in direct competition with his.

That didn't strike him as normal and got Virgil thinking he might've missed something.

Arriving home, he found Cora and Jack curled up on the couch sleeping. Obviously they'd had an emotionally exhausting day and he didn't want to disturb them.

He called Ethan to bring him up to date on the school fire and advised him to be on his guard all night then he went into the kitchen and fixed a simple dinner. Afterwards, he bent down and kissed Cora on the cheek. Her eyes fluttered open.

"Dinner's ready."

She instantly sat up and looked at her watch. "My goodness, where did the time go?" Looking down at a still slumbering Jack, she smiled. "I was thinking what I'd do if anything ever happened to him."

Virgil put his hand on her arm. "We'll make sure it doesn't."

Their gazes met and she said, "You know we can't prevent danger from snatching him from us."

"We can do everything possible to keep him safe."

Tears welled in her eyes. "He means so much to us. If only we could have other children."

Virgil knelt and cupped her face in the palms of his hands. "He's all we need."

Jack stirred and sat up, his knuckles digging into his eyes. "What time is it? I'm hungry."

They gathered at the table and Cora glanced at his miserable failure at a decent meal. Forgoing the hot dogs, Virgil tried his hand at goulash. Not only did it look a mess but, when he tasted it, he could hardly swallow.

Cora took a small bite and immediately removed the pan from the table, put it back on the stove, added some spices and a jar of tomatoes and before he could get Jack's milk poured, and the coffee cups full, dinner was back on the table smelling delicious.

Virgil carefully took a spoonful then grinned. "You're so much better at this than I am."

"I appreciate you trying."

Looking at the back door, Virgil said, "Where is Earl?"

"I think he's having dinner with a friend then going to the town hall meeting."

Virgil blinked. "I've already forgotten about that. I better hurry."

"If it's okay, I think Jack and I will stay home."

"That's a good idea. We're hoping to get some volunteers to help patrol the city. I don't want you doing that."

Finishing dinner, he shoved back his chair, got up and leaned over to capture her lips. "Wait up for me." He winked. "I won't be long."

Everyone had already gathered in the hall when Virgil arrived. He took his seat at the head of the room with Mayor McBride and the council. Carl and Buford were there, along with the people whose businesses had been affected by the fires. Looking to the right, he saw Eddie and two of his three sons. He assumed, like Carl and Buford, Eddie had left someone behind to watch their business.

The mayor started off by telling everyone about the fires and how their help was needed if they wanted to prevent any more damage.

Ben Welsh stood. "I'm worried about my business being hit next. People in this town need a drug store."

Virgil looked out at the concerned faces. "I'd like to tell you I know where this maniac will hit next, but I can't. That's why we need men willing to walk the streets day and night until this guy is caught."

Arthur stood. "Have you found any clues or evidence that might help you figure out who's behind this?"

Virgil shook his head. "Not really. There doesn't seem to be a reason for this happening. They certainly aren't trying to rob anyone."

Frank stood up. "Virgil, Ethan and I have been over the fires with a fine-toothed comb. We've even had an expert from Joplin advising us on the case. There's nothing linking anyone to these fires." He held out his hands. "But, we're dealing with a dangerous individual. If we don't stop him, no one in Gibbs City will be safe."

"Do they want to destroy the town? Could they have a grudge against someone? Or perhaps it's an outsider."

"Those are all good points, Arnie. But, I don't have the answer. Several people were close enough to the fire in the barbershop to notice if someone had driven away. So, I think the person we're looking for lives here. We think he's a young, athletic man. That's about all we have to go on."

"What can we do?" Carl asked.

"I need men who can take four hour shifts, day or night. This way the town is being watched at all times." Several hands were held up and voices rose above the crowd. "There's a place where you can sign up over there on that table. Ethan will answer your questions."

"What about our businesses?"

"I suggest you hire extra people to guard your place at night, but remember, Leonard's property was set on fire in the middle of the day and his wife was home."

Groans filled the air. "We can't keep living like this."

"Sheriff, you need to do something."

"I'm doing all I can with the manpower I have. I'm there every day trying to find the responsible party. I need you doing the same thing."

"Fire! Fire! The grocery store is on fire."

Virgil, Ethan and Frank ran out of the door and toward Glover's Market. Frank jumped into his car. "I'm going to get the truck, I'll be right back."

Virgil and Ethan ran toward the store and around the back. There was more smoke than fire. Desperate to keep the fire from growing, Virgil emptied out several bags of potatoes and he and Ethan began beating the flames with the burlap sacks.

Buckets of water appeared and men scrambled to do what they could while women huddled safely away from harm.

Frank and his crew raced down Main Street with the truck siren blaring. Once he arrived, and the hoses were unrolled, the fire was out in no time.

His nostrils on fire and the blisters on his hands bleeding, Virgil leaned against a telephone pole, removed his hat and wiped his brow. "Who wasn't at the meeting?"

"Every businessperson in town was there. Even Caroline's mother, Josephine," Ethan said.

"What about residents?"

Carl came rushing over. "I checked and every business in town was accounted for. Buford went to the station should anyone get the idea we're distracted by the fire here and won't be paying attention."

"Good idea." Virgil went over to Howard. "I'm sorry about this mess. It looks like you didn't lose too much, but the building may not be safe for customers."

"My wife was upstairs just like Leonard's. She could've been sleeping and died of smoke inhalation."

Virgil rested a hand on his shoulder. "I know. Please believe me, Howard, I'm doing everything I can to catch this guy. Tomorrow Gene McKinnon, an FBI agent, will be coming to see me. Maybe he'll have some advice."

"Good, in the meantime, I'm going to need some help cleaning this up and nailing plywood over the windows to keep looters away."

"We'll all pitch in."

"Jesus, what's this world coming to?"

CHAPTER THIRTEEN

Cora hated leaving Gibbs City with Virgil so busy trying to catch the arsonist, but she felt in her heart that this had to be done. No matter how cruelly her mother had treated her, she couldn't bring herself to return the coldness.

She and Earl had arrived in St. Louis Monday morning. Her mother's sentencing was set for three in the afternoon. After freshening up, they made their way through the busy sidewalk traffic to the county jail where her mother was being held.

They entered the building and Cora's body automatically tensed and she couldn't breathe. She hated the smell of this place, the taste of it coated her tongue and the sounds vibrated loudly through her ears.

Walking to the desk, she placed her hand on the counter and asked, "May I see Clare Williams?"

The sergeant opened a large, hardcover ledger and ran his pudgy finger down the row of names. "Oh, there she is." He turned and looked at the large, round clock on the walk. "She's due in court in a couple of hours."

"I was wondering if I might speak to her before." Cora captured his attention. "I'm her daughter."

He nodded toward Earl. "Who's he?"

"Don't you clutter up your mind with who I am." He pointed to Cora. "I'm here with her."

"That don't mean you get to go back there."

"I will or you'll answer to Malcom Ryall."

The sergeant straightened. "I haven't heard that name in a long time." He leaned across the counter, looked around then whispered. "Is he still alive?"

"Breathing as good as me and you. Now let us in before I lose my patience."

It amazed her how quickly the heavy man moved. Not only that, he tipped his head politely to her as she passed. Earl, the greatest mystery of Gibbs City and now of St. Louis, too.

"So, who is Malcom Ryall?"

"Just a friend I know. Nothing to worry your sweet head about."

They waited on the opposite side of a rectangular table as her mother, shackled, and dressed in a black and white stripped shift, was led into the room. Cora stood while Earl remained seated.

Her mother, none too pleased at Earl's lack of manners, snarled. "Who's he?"

"A very dear friend."

Arrogant as ever, Clare lifted her nose. "Is he house broken?"

Earl placed his hat on the table and leaner closer. "I'm about as good as you're going to get. So put your ass in the chair. You make one move to touch Cora and I'll kill you before the guard over there knows what's going on."

Eyes narrowed in suspicion, her mother took the seat across from her. "I'm glad you came."

"I hate to think what will happen to you, Mother."

"I don't expect it to be a picnic."

Her mother had absolutely no idea about the horrors of prison. The things they could do to you, the pain they could inflict, and the fear they could instill in your mind.

"Virgil says he doubts they'll give you the electric chair."

"My attorney thinks the same thing, but who can guess the mood of a judge?"

"Life in prison can be a death sentence in itself."

"I'm aware of that." Her mother looked around the room. "I don't know if you noticed or not, but this certainly isn't the Ritz."

"It is compared to prison."

Her mother paled and pleated her fingers together. "I know."

"Is there anything we can do to help?"

Her mother's face contorted into an annoyed grimace. "Probably not."

"I'll be at the hearing and I promise to visit you in prison."

"Why would you do that, Missy?" Earl scowled. "She never gave you the time of day."

"How do you know," Clare Williams demanded. "You have no idea the pain I suffered when she was in prison."

"Then why didn't you do anything to get her out of that hellhole?"

"My husband said she was being well cared for. He paid Warden Becker to make sure they treated her kindly."

"He wasn't paying off the warden. They were racketeering together." Earl's voice rose. "Where'd you think all those minks and diamonds came from?"

"I'd assumed my husband was conducting a legitimate business."

"Well," Earl gritted out, practically crawling over the table. "He made his money prostituting his own daughter. Her sweat and tears gave you everything you've had for the last five years."

"Earl, please," Cora begged. "I don't honestly think she knew."

He sat back, his eyes hard. "She knew all there was to know. That doesn't explain why she didn't bother to visit you at least once. Unnatural, is what I say."

"I wasn't as clever as you think, Mr. Earl. Robert was a master manipulator. I was an innocent pawn."

When Earl went to contradict her, Clare held up her hand. "I'm not saying I'm the nicest person in the world, or even kind. But I swear, I knew nothing about what went on in that place."

"Well, now you're fixing to find out."

Her mother tilted her head. "Yes, I am and regardless of what happens, I have to live with knowing that I didn't do more about Eleanor's murder."

"Your testimony put Father in jail."

Her mother looked away. "He's where he belongs."

"And Judge Martin?"

"I don't regret for one minute that I shot that man. He was a monster." Her mother's face softened. "How is Jack?"

Earl turned away. "Wouldn't you like to know?"

"Yes, I would. Very much."

Cora smiled. "He's doing wonderfully. Growing taller and stronger every day."

"You married?"

"Yes, Sheriff Virgil Carter."

A rare smiled tilted her mother's mouth. "You look happy."

"I've never felt like this."

Her mother grasped her hands. "I'm happy for you. If there is anyone who deserves the very best in this world, it's you, Cora."

"Thank you." Cora wasn't sure what to make of her mother's sudden interest.

The guard came over. "I'm sorry, but your time is up."

With a man on each side, they escorted her mother back to her cell. Earl looked at her and pointed his finger. "Don't you dare cry. That woman turned her back on you and Jack. I don't believe her for one minute."

"Maybe she didn't know."

"You think that kept her from visiting you? Sending you a birthday card? Being there waiting when you got out?"

Cora lowered her head. "No, she didn't do any of that."

"And that was all her choice."

"I know, but something in my heart reaches out to her. Maybe because she's still my mother, maybe somewhere in my mind are happier times, maybe I can forgive easier than you."

"It's not about forgiving, Missy. It's about protecting yourself from people who can and will hurt you. I wouldn't put a lot of trust in her sudden change of heart."

They left for a quick lunch before leaving for the courthouse. Cora hated seeing her mother sentenced to a life of hell, but there was nothing she could do but be there for her.

They sat in the first pew and waited. They were early and the room was empty. She'd just turned to Earl when Dan Martin walked up and stopped in front of her. His face was a mask of anger and rage.

"So, you came to see the bitch hang."

Cora sat up. "I don't think they hang anyone nowadays."

"They should."

Earl placed his body between them. "Who's this fool?"

"Judge Martin's son."

Earl looked Dan up and down. "Well, it doesn't appear the apple fell far from the tree."

Dan reached out to grab Earl, but quick as a bullet, Earl grabbed his hand and bent it backward until Dan fell to the floor in agony.

Picking up his hat, Dan came to his feet quickly, his face bright, his jaw tight. "Who the hell are you?"

"Don't you worry about that. You stay away from her. You hear?"

"She has my son."

Earl leaned closer. "You ain't got no son and if you come sniffing around, you'll be six feet under."

The bailiff opened a door from the back of the room. Cora watched her mother shuffle in behind another officer. Her drab, gray dress and ugly shoes were a far cry from the designer wardrobe she once owned. She never looked so miserable with no comb to fix her hair and no make-up or lotion. What a difference a few months could make.

The guard escorted her to the defendant's table and removed the heavy chains. After seeing her settled in the chair, he moved to stand directly behind her. She quickly glanced back and their gazes locked.

Cora knew exactly how her mother felt. Alone, frightened, and unsure what would happen to her.

The lawyers came in and then the bailiff announced the judge to the front of the courtroom. Since her mother had pleaded guilty, there hadn't been much of a trial.

Judge McElroy looked stern with his bushy brows low and his mouth firmly set. "Mrs. Clare Williams, it is the duty of this court to sentence you for the crime of murdering Judge Albert Martin."

"We understand," her attorney said.

"Do you have anything to add?" the judge asked.

Her mother shook her head.

"Nothing that would induce this court for leniency?"

The lawyer came to his feet. "Your honor, Mrs. Williams admits to shooting Judge Martin. He was a corrupt, brutal man who deserved to die, but my client will accept whatever the court mandates."

The judge flipped through several papers and then looked up. "Is there anyone in the room who can speak for the character of Mrs. Williams?"

The attorney looked at Cora. "Her daughter is here, sir."

"Please step forward."

Cora stood on shaking knees. One glance at the frown on Earl's face relayed he didn't think there should be any mercy.

Cora was asked to approach the judge.

"Your name?"

"Cora Carter."

"Do you believe your mother should be sentenced to death?"

"I don't think anyone should be given the electric chair. Especially for shooting the man who killed her daughter."

Dan Martin jumped to his feet. "Your Honor, that was my father. He was a good man who did numerous good deeds for this city and his businesses provided a lot of jobs."

"That's true, Mr. Martin."

Cora licked her lips. "But, I'd also like to bring it to the attention of the court that he was prostituting prisoners, throwing extravagant parties for his wealthy friends there and drugs were always available."

"None of that was proven in a court of law," Dan shouted.

"It didn't need to be, Mr. Martin," the judge said. "We all knew it."

"Also, there is the charge of racketeering."

"Again," Dan shouted and his face turned red. "You're putting a dead man on trial."

The judge leaned forward. "That's not what we're doing here, young man. We're simply explaining why Mrs. Williams was driven to murder your father."

"Because she's a snooty bitch."

"That's enough." He pointed his gavel at Dan. "You take a seat and stay in it before I have you removed."

"Clare Williams, please stand."

Cora looked back and noticed her mother's hands shook. She glanced at Cora and tried to smile.

"Mrs. Clare Williams, I sentence you to a minimum security facility in Jefferson City, Missouri for ten years."

Cora's knees nearly buckled from relief. How had they gotten so lucky? She looked at the judge who smiled briefly before leaving the courtroom. Earl met her near the table where her mother stood in disbelief.

"I'm shocked," her mother said.

"You should be," the lawyer remarked, closing his briefcase. "I thought the very least you'd get would be life."

"You'll be okay, Mother. That place is so much better than the Missouri State Penitentiary for Women. You'll even be able to get out early on good behavior."

"You mean I could be locked up less than the sentence?"

"Yes, if you obey the rules and keep to yourself."

Her mother's chin shivered through a shaky smile. "I can hardly believe my luck."

Dan rushed over. "You better hope they keep you locked up because if I see you walking the street, I'll kill you myself."

Earl pushed him away. "You better watch what you say. There are witnesses who overheard you threatening her life."

"I don't care." Dan slammed his hat on his head and pointed at Cora. His eyes were narrowed with hatred. "And I'm going to take Jack away from you."

Earl jumped between them. "You just try." He took Cora by the arm and led her out of the courthouse. She couldn't catch her breath. Her knees felt weak and her mouth was dry as cotton. Her pounding heart drowned out Earl's voice.

Dear God, the thought of losing Jack nearly paralyzed her with fear. She had to talk to Virgil. She had to warn him. What if Dan tried something while she was away? While Virgil was trying to find an arsonist, and while she and her husband were struggling to create a future.

"Take me to the hotel, Earl. I need to call Virgil."

"Now, listen, Missy. People like Dan Martin talk big, but they're usually all bark and no bite. Don't go worrying about something before you have a reason."

She stopped abruptly and turned to face him. "We're talking about Jack. Any threat against him is a threat to everything I hold dear. Losing Jack would destroy me. He means everything to me. I love him with all my heart. He's my son."

Earl took her arms and spoke gently. "I know all that. But, don't fret when you don't have a cause yet. Dan may just be blowing off steam because they didn't send your mother to the electric chair."

She bit her bottom lip. "You could be right, but I plan to let Virgil know."

"Good idea. You do that then we'll grab some coffee and pie."

"I'm still full from lunch."

"And I think you'll want to say goodbye to your mother."

"Yes." She placed her hands on his chest. "I forgot about that as well." She rubbed her forehead. "The mention of Dan taking Jack took over my mind completely."

"I understand. Let's get back to the hotel and you call Virgil."

CHAPTER FOURTEEN

Virgil had just come in from searching every square inch of Gibbs City for the maniac setting fire to his town when the phone rang. He hadn't slept since Cora left because this mess with the fires had to be stopped. People were talking about closing down their businesses and leaving town.

"Hello."

"Virgil," Cora said in a voice too high and filled with panic.

"What's wrong?"

"Dan has threatened to take Jack."

"You have legal guardianship. That'll hold up in court."

"But, what if he just takes him away and we can't find him?"

"That's not going to happen. I'll put a few guys watching the school and I'll contact Batcher to put a tail on Martin. He heads this way, we'll know quick enough."

She let out a deep sigh. "I'm so frightened."

"I know, sweetheart. But, it's probably more talk than Dan actually doing anything."

"That's what Earl said."

"Listen to him." Virgil knew that the piece of paper Cora had held little value when it came to taking a child away from a parent but he could never tell her that. The judicial system usually

109

favored the parents no matter the circumstances. But he couldn't bring himself to tell her. "What happened at your mother's hearing?"

"Good news. The judge sentenced her to ten years in a minimum security facility. She might get out in seven years."

Virgil wanted Clare locked away from Cora for the rest of her life. "What's so great about that?"

A long silence filled the moment. "She actually asked about my life and Jack. Maybe she's changing. At least I won't be worrying my head off."

That was true. He knew Cora and how she felt about people suffering. "I'm sorry. It's just I wished she'd been that considerate toward you."

"That's the past, Virgil. At least now I know she's going to be okay."

"What are your plans?"

"Earl and I are grabbing a snack. A piece of pie, of course. After that I'll say goodbye to mother, then we're catching the afternoon bus back home."

"Good, I've missed you and want you here safe with me."

"Any news on who's setting the fires."

Virgil ran his hands through his hair. "Not a damned thing. I'm completely stumped. Gene McKinnon is coming tomorrow. Maybe he'll have some ideas."

"Okay, I love you. See you soon."

"Be careful."

Virgil went to Maggie's and picked up Jack. Mrs. Winters had come down with a cold and couldn't babysit Jack while Cora was gone, so Maggie had stepped in.

He'd planned for them to go to Betty's Diner for a burger and fries. Cora would throw a fit if she knew the way they'd been eating since she left. No home cooked meals unless Maggie came up with them.

After investigating all day, he wasn't interested in cooking. Besides, as soon as they finished supper and listened to Jack's program, they were off to bed in minutes. While Jack slept soundly, Virgil had laid awake late into the night.

The boy grumbled about the play time being canceled. Then he suddenly remembered the new loose tooth he'd discovered. "Looky here, I can wiggle it around."

Grinning, Virgil admired the front tooth and relaxed for the first time in days. He knew it wouldn't' last, but it felt good to share a child's innocent enthusiasm. "Looks like the tooth fairy will be paying us a visit."

They drove to the diner and ordered. Maybe Cora wouldn't be happy, but Jack was delighted. He tore into his burger like a boy who'd gone hungry for days. Tossing some cash on the table, he and Jack bundled up against the cold anxious to get home. Jack didn't want to miss his radio program before they had to pick Cora and Earl up at the bus station.

He'd just turned on the radio when a knock sounded at the door. Arthur stood on the porch, his hat in his hand.

"Come in," Virgil said. "Cora's out of town so I can't offer you anything but coffee."

"That would be wonderful on a cold night like this."

Virgil put on the coffee, motioned for Arthur to join him in the kitchen while Jack stayed occupied with his program. Waiting for the brew to cool, Virgil asked, "What brings you out?"

"I'm worried about these fires."

"We all are."

"I'm wondering if it's retaliation from that gang of bootleggers Bart was tied up with in Kansas."

"Why would they burn businesses?"

"Well, you shut down their supply lines and I got word they're hurting for booze."

Virgil thought for a few minutes. "That could be a reason to come after me, but not the whole town."

"What if they want to shut down Gibbs City?"

"That wouldn't improve their chances of getting more liquor."

Arthur looked tired and anxious, like so many other business owners in town. "I know, but I can't believe anyone in Gibbs City would do this. Do you?"

Virgil set his cup down. "I don't know what to believe anymore. These fires are random and dangerous. Who sets a fire where people are inside? Leonard and Howard's wives could've been killed."

"I'm thinking we might be smart to set a trap."

Virgil liked the sound of that, but at the same time, it could be very dangerous. "Go on."

"You know I own several businesses in town. At least the buildings they're in. What if we made a couple of my properties look mighty tempting to the person setting the fires?"

"How would we go about that?"

"Well, I own the furniture store right off of Main Street. Everett Roth runs it for me, but what if I send him to Joplin for a few days and we left the building unmanned."

"You do realize that if we misjudge, you could lose a lot of money?"

Arthur stood and paced as he nibbled on his thumbnail. "What else can we do?" He stopped and looked at Virgil. "We have to stop this before the town falls apart. People are already talking about not renewing their leases, selling out and moving to other towns. Now the safety of our children is at stake."

"I agree with everything you're saying, but you stand to lose the most."

"I'm willing to take that chance."

Virgil stood. "Let me think about it. Talk to a few people, but keep it under our hats."

Arthur held out his hand. "Agreed."

"We'll meet tomorrow at the judge's office. The FBI agent, Gene McKinnon is going to be there. We can always use his expertise."

Arthur nodded, put his coat and hat on and left.

"Jack, put your coat on. It's time to pick up Aunt Cora. The bus should be arriving soon and I don't want them waiting."

They left and headed toward the bus station. The bus from St. Louis had just arrived and the driver was opening the luggage area when Virgil parked and he and Jack went to meet Cora and Earl.

She saw him and ran into his arms. Holding her felt wonderful and his chest loosened a little. Not having her home was damned hard on his heart. Funny how the craziest things can run through a man's head.

"You catch the person trying to burn down the town?" Earl asked.

Virgil shook his head as he relieved Earl of the two suitcases and put them in the trunk. Shivering, everyone hurried into the car. "But I think we might have come up with a plan."

"Really?" Cora asked. "I hope it doesn't put your life in danger. Nothing is worth you getting hurt."

Virgil loved the way she looked, how her eyes sparkled. Just being near her made his heart race. She sat in the back seat of the car holding Jack. "Everyone will be okay if we can pull it off."

"Well, what is it?" Earl insisted. "What are you cooking up?"

"It's actually Arthur's idea. He, like so many others, is sick of all the uncertainty, so we're thinking of setting a trap."

Earl chuckled. "I like that."

"I'll know more tomorrow, but for now, keep it under your hat."

"You can count on me," Earl said. "It will feel good to sleep in my own bed tonight."

Cora chuckled. "He slept most of the way home."

"Did not. How could I with that brat behind me kicking my seat?"

"Believe me, you managed."

They arrived home, said goodnight to Earl and Virgil heated up the leftover coffee he and Arthur had shared. "You hungry?"

"No, we stopped and Earl and I grabbed a sandwich. But that coffee smells good."

"We ate at Betty's Diner all the time you were gone," Jack said with a smile. "I sure love hamburgers."

Cora slid him a disapproving glare. "I suspected as much."

113

"Well, Uncle Virgil can cook, but he ain't that good."

"Hey now, you want hot dogs Saturday or not?"

Jack smiled and ran to his room with Pal right behind him. "Oh boy! Hot dogs."

Cora crossed her arms. "I can just imagine all the crazy food you two have been eating. Did you at least fix breakfast and make sure Jack had a glass of milk?"

"Yes, I did."

"Well, that's good news."

The Virgil and Jack shed their coats while she removed her hat and put her purse away. Virgil poured two cups of coffee and then Jack came in to say goodnight.

Cora squeezed him extra tight and smothered his face with kisses until Jack struggled to get out of her grasp. She looked at him. "Since when have you been so big I can't get all the sugar I want?"

"I ain't no little boy anymore. I can't have you kissing all over me. Tommy would be laughing his fool head off if he saw us."

Cora put her hand on his shoulder. "I'll have you know I get all the kisses I want and no one can stop me." She tapped him on the nose. "And stop saying ain't. There's no such word."

"Then why does everyone say it?"

"They don't know better. You do."

"Oh, guess what, Aunt Cora?" Excitement brightened the young boy's face. "I got a loose tooth." Using his tongue he wiggled his front tooth. "That means I'm going to get rich from the tooth fairy."

"Be sure to save it when it falls out. Do you want Uncle Virgil to help you and pull it?"

Jack sealed his lips together, slapped his hands over his mouth and shook his head.

"Okay, we'll wait. Meanwhile, brush the teeth that will be in your mouth for a while then put your pajamas on."

After Jack went to bed, Cora moved to sit on Virgil's lap and leaned her head on his shoulder. "I'm exhausted but I feel going was the right thing to do."

He rubbed her back. "If you're happy then I am, too."

Propping her chin on his shoulder, she said, "Now I'm worried about Dan."

"Don't be." Virgil lowered his voice. "He doesn't want Jack. He's just trying to get you all riled up." He shifted, put his finger beneath her chin and lifted her face. "Looks like he succeeded."

"Jack means everything, Virgil."

"Yes, he does and I won't let anything happen to him."

"But we're not with him twenty-four hours a day."

"No kid can grow up like that. Dan's angry and he's letting off steam, but he knows better than to come here and cause trouble."

She touched his arm. "But you will call David Batcher, won't you?"

"I'm calling him first thing in the morning." He leaned closer and captured her lips. The warmth of her touch sped up his heartrate and had him wanting more. He picked her up and carried her to the bedroom and placed her on the bed.

Leaving for a few minutes he locked the door, turned out the lights and joined Cora. Time for all their worries to melt away.

CHAPTER FIFTEEN

Cora went to work the following day with a lighter heart. Her mother would be in a far better place than a state prison. Nothing good happened there. Before reaching her office, she ran into Stan and told him the news from St. Louis.

"Has Virgil found out anything about who's setting the fires?"

"That seems to be on everyone's mind lately." She touched the doctor's arm. "He's doing all he can. At least last night was quiet"

"I worry that one of the citizens is going to be injured or killed. Leonard's wife was lucky. We can't expect the same results if this continues."

Cora didn't want to say anything about Virgil having a plan even though she knew Stan could be trusted. If this plan, whatever it was, was going to work, it had to be kept a secret.

She went to her office and caught up on her paperwork after being away from work for two days. Then she checked on her patients to find two ready to be discharged.

At the nurse's station, she talked to the staff and instructed them to make sure they had plenty of supplies should anything happen. She didn't like fires and it would be a shame if the hospital was caught unprepared.

As she moved back to her office, the alarm went off. There was an emergency. She ran to the bottom floor to find Henry from the hardware store being wheeled in on a gurney.

She quickly opened a room for him.

Virgil had brought him in. "His place was set on fire and he tried to put out the flames."

"We'll take care of him."

"I have to get back."

"Go," she shouted.

Screaming in pain, Henry's eyes met hers. "Get that bitch away from me. She ain't touching me. I want a real doctor."

Dr. Adams came in and assured Henry that only he would be attending to his condition. Stunned, Cora backed away. How could a doctor act so callously? "That's my patient."

"He wants nothing to do with you and I don't blame him," Dr. Adams hissed. "Now go find something else to do while I stabilize Henry."

Cora glanced at the assisting Nurse Hill and saw the satisfied smirk on her face. Unsure what to do or how to react, she turned to leave. Stan walked into the room.

"What's going on here?"

"This patient doesn't want Dr. Carter. He's insisted I take care of him."

Stan looked at Nurse Hill and Dr. Adams then stepped between them. "Leave the room immediately. You too, Nurse Hill. This is Dr. Carter's patient and he'll either accept her, or he can suffer until we can transfer him to Joplin."

"But he doesn't want her."

"That's not his choice. She's the emergency room physician today and that means you can't bully your way in here and take over."

He took the doctor by the arm and escorted him from the room. Cora swung into action by ordering pain medication and linen bandages. The medication made Henry too drowsy to make a fuss. The burns were limited to his hands, arms and feet. The next thing she knew, Nurse Hill was replaced by another RN and Cora had Henry taken to a room.

Stan waited in the corridor. "I'm sorry for that, Cora."

"It's not your fault. I'm afraid Henry isn't too fond of me. For some reason he blames me for ruining his hardware business."

"That's still no way for Adams to behave." He ran his fingers through his hair. "And frankly, I've had it with Nurse Hill. Her attitude is horrible. We've received enough complaints about her to see she never works in another hospital."

"I would say I'm sorry to hear that, but I'm not. She's overstepped her authority too many times."

"How is Henry?"

"His hands and forearms are pretty bad, but while I was examining him I noticed his feet were burned as well."

"Fire does strange things. Sometimes it has a mind of its own."

"I think I'll still bring it to Virgil's attention."

After making sure Henry was comfortable and the pain under control, Cora went to her office and called Virgil. He wasn't there, but she left a message for him to come to the hospital if he had a chance.

Within an hour he walked toward her, a worried expression on his face. She'd asked Frank to join him and, from the looks of both men, they'd barely taken the time to wash up.

"Why did you need us?" Virgil asked.

"You're going to think I'm crazy, but something isn't right."

"Really, what?" Frank asked. His face was tight and drawn. "What are we talking about?"

Cora led them to Henry's room. The medication had him out cold. "Henry has burns on his hands and arms."

"He got that from fighting the fire," Virgil stated.

She pulled back the sheets to expose his feet. "Then why are there burns on the tops of his feet?"

Virgil looked closer. "On the tops."

Frank scratched his head. "Those should be on the bottoms of his feet."

Cora turned to the two men. "Unless he set the fire and some of the fuel he used spilled onto his shoes when he was pouring it out." She pointed to a pair of charred work boots in the corner. "They reek of kerosene."

The two men stared at each other, a knowing expression covered their blackened faces. "You think Henry is our arsonist?"

Virgil shook his head. "I don't know. He's a lot older than the description we have. The arsonist is a fast runner, too."

"He could've been doing this to punish the townsfolk for shopping at the new hardware store."

Rubbing the back of his neck, Virgil said, "That would make sense and we all know he's mean as a snake."

Frank looked at Henry lying unconscious. "But, why such drastic measures?"

"We'll wait until he's awake and find out."

Virgil left and Cora went back to her office. As she prepared to break for lunch, Dr. Adams walked up to her. For a moment she thought he might want to apologize.

"You're such a troublemaker," he accused. "No one wants a woman doctor. I certainly don't. I'm going to get you fired if it's the last thing I do."

"Go ahead. But the next time you interfere between me and a patient, I won't need Dr. Lowery to stop you, I'll take it to the board."

"I wouldn't be so fast there. You're barely out of the woods. One wrong move and they'll remove you like that." Dr. Adams snapped his fingers. "No one wants you anyway."

"That's only your opinion."

"Oh, there are others. They're just not saying anything out loud."

"Do what you want. I'm here to stay."

"I hope no accidents happen, Cora."

A chill ran down her spine and Cora shivered. She turned and stabbed him with a hard glare. "Are you threatening me, Dr. Adams."

"Not at all."

"Good, because that would be the last thing you ever do."

"I'm not afraid of your husband."

"Then you haven't been paying attention."

CHAPTER SIXTEEN

Virgil met Arthur, Gene and Ethan in Judge Garner's chambers right after lunch. As the men took seats and settled back, the judge spoke first. "Arthur, I want to tell you right up front that I don't like this idea of a trap. God only knows what could go wrong."

Virgil sat up, running his finger around the brim of his hat. "Cora called me to the hospital this morning. Henry was hurt when his hardware store was set on fire."

"I heard he tried to put out the fire," Ethan said. "A man has to try to save what he's got."

"The only problem is Frank and I think he might've set the fire."

Arthur blinked. "Really?"

"Why?" asked the judge. "That's his livelihood."

"You think he's our arsonist?" Ethan asked.

Virgil held up his hands. "I haven't talked to Henry yet, and until I do, everything is just us guessing." He cleared his throat. "Gene did a little checking around and learned that Henry was at the honky tonk the night the feed store burned. That leads us to think that maybe he torched his own place to make it look like the arsonist did it to get the insurance money."

"Yes," Arthur said, stroking his chin. "He's been going downhill since Anderson's moved in. Good reason to get out and have a little cash to boot."

Ethan put his elbows on his knees. "But why did he burn himself?"

Virgil looked at the judge. "My guess is it wasn't as easy as he thought. Some kerosene spilled on his shoes and he didn't notice before striking the match and his shoes caught on fire. He panicked."

Arthur tightened his lips. "If that's the way it went down, then he got what he deserves."

"I agree," said the judge. "The bad thing is our guy is still out there."

"Yes, and Henry played right into his hands."

Leaning back and releasing a sigh, the judged packed his pipe with tobacco, struck a match, and inhaled. "What's the plan?"

"Thought you didn't like it," Arthur said.

"I don't, but we need to stop this before someone dies."

"As I told Virgil, I can send Roth to Joplin and leave the furniture store closed a few days. We can hide inside and surround the outside and wait. That might be too tempting for our guy not to strike."

"What if someone inside gets killed?"

"We'll use two-way radios," Gene offered. "I can get all we need."

Judge Garner dipped his head. "I know this isn't in your jurisdiction and I appreciate your help, Gene."

"The important thing is we catch the guy. Once he's behind bars, we'll work the rest out," Gene said.

"Your superiors don't mind?"

"No, they want crime stopped wherever we find it."

The judge took a drag off his pipe. "When do you want to try this scheme of yours?"

Arthur sat forward. "Not on the weekend. There are too many people out and about, but what about the first of next week. I'll start spreading the news and put a sign out that the furniture store will be closed Monday and Tuesday due to inventory."

"We might be able to lure the arsonist out," Virgil said. "I worry about Arthur's business if the guy strikes and we don't catch him. But I feel we have to do something and this is as good as anything else we've come up with."

Ethan stood and walked to the window. "We've been prowling the streets of Gibbs City like a hungry alley cat and we've come up with nothing."

Virgil looked at Gene. "Can you take Henry's boots to your office and have them run a test to determine if it's kerosene?"

Gene nodded. "I can get the results back to you by Monday."

The judge leaned back. "I appreciate all you can do. Virgil, be careful interrogating Henry. If he's our guy, I don't want him spooked. If he set that fire to his place on purpose, he's as guilty as the arsonist. Tread carefully."

"I will. First, I want to hear Gene's test results."

"When you described his injuries to me it sounded suspicious. Then we found most of his expensive items in a shed outside his home. That makes me think it was deliberate."

Ethan walked back and sat down. "I agree. But, he was awful careless. He could've been burned alive."

"I don't think he figured it was that hard."

"Well, I hope he learned his lesson."

They left and Arthur went back to the dry cleaners, Ethan went home to get some sleep and Gene came to Virgil's office.

"I heard your wife went to her mother's sentencing hearing?"

Virgil put on a fresh pot of coffee. "Lord, don't get me started on that."

"After all her parents did to her."

"Those were my words, exactly. But, if it helps Cora deal with the past, then I'll keep my mouth shut."

"Best you do. No man alive can figure out the workings of a woman's mind."

Virgil laughed. He loved Cora and only wanted what made her happy. "While she and our neighbor were there, Dan Martin threatened to take Jack away."

Gene looked at him with intuitive eyes. "You think he means it?"

"I don't know. If he tries, I'll kill him."

"Doesn't she have legal custody?"

"Yes, but we all know that might not stand up in a court of law."

"It would here, in Gibbs City."

"But, if Dan could get everything done in St. Louis, I honestly don't think Cora would stand a chance."

Gene poured two cups of coffee. "Let's hope he doesn't come and take the child. It would be hard to get him back."

"I've let the school know that Jack's not to be released to anyone they don't know. Batcher is keeping a close eye on Dan's movements in St. Louis. If he heads this way, I'll be waiting."

Gene sat in Ethan's chair. "After the trial, I went through everything we had hoping to find something the FBI could pin on Dan. We all know he's as involved as his father was, but we don't have a shred of evidence."

"We were all shocked when Dan walked away from all that free of anything. I understand he's living in his father's house and could be continuing the family business."

"I checked that out and couldn't find a single thing that would lead me to open an investigation."

Virgil hated to ask, but he had to know exactly where the whole situation stood. "What are your superiors saying, Gene. They want you to back off?"

Gene shook his head. "Naw, my boss is a pretty tough character. Came up through the ranks and can be a hard-nosed son of a bitch when it comes to bringing down organized crime."

Virgil smiled. "Good, those are my favorite kind of people."

Gene drained his cup and stood. "I thought so. I'm heading back to Joplin. You hear anything, let me know. How is the arson investigator working out?"

"I just notified him of Henry's store burning and my suspicions. He's damned good at what he does. A few hours at the scene and I think he can tell us exactly what happened."

"Frank's pretty good at that, too."

"He's been around fires all his life. His daddy was a fireman. Frank knows the behavior of flames and he can spot the point of origin the minute the fire's out."

"Good, keep me posted."

Virgil watched Gene walk away and thought about all the problems on his plate. Someone wanted to burn down his town and Dan wanted to rip out Cora's heart. His as well. He couldn't have a son he'd think more of than Jack. And he'd wade through anything to keep him. Dan Martin had no idea who he was messing with.

Looking at the clock, Virgil left to go pick up Jack and Tommy from school. If Susan hadn't picked up Ronnie, he'd give the three boys a lift home. After Dan's threats, Virgil wasn't taking any chances.

When he arrived, he saw Earl, standing near the door, bundled up in his coat. Virgil rolled the squad car up next to him. "What are you doing here?"

Earl turned to look at him. "Picking up Jack."

"Why, is something wrong?"

"I didn't know you were getting him." Earl leaned down and propped his forearms on the open window. "After listening to Dan Martin flap his jaws, I'm not taking any chances. I'm making sure Jack gets home safely."

Virgil motioned for Earl to get into the car. "Come on, I'll drive everyone home."

His neighbor opened the car and slid in. "Do you pick him up every day?"

"Either I do or Maggie does." He smiled at the older man. "You becoming Jack's protector?"

"I ain't sitting by and letting nothing happen to that boy. He's like my own and I won't let Missy suffer through losing him."

"I've spoken to the school. They won't let Dan have Jack."

"But what if he's waiting out here for him to get out of school?"

"Maggie and I are always here."

"Good, because I don't like the way the bastard looked at Cora. Like all he wanted to do was hurt her."

"She's been through a lot. One of the detectives that I know in St. Louis is keeping an eye on Dan. He heads this way we'll know."

"You think that will stop him."

"It should, if he has any brains at all."

Earl stared at the door the children would soon be spilling out of. "I don't trust him."

"Neither do I."

Earl looked at him quickly. "What about Henry's place going up in flames?"

"I think the thick-headed tyrant might have burned down the place."

"Really?" Earl returned to his vigil. "That's pretty crazy."

"Everything is screwed up lately. If, for a fact, Henry did set that fire, then he's not the arsonist and I still have a problem on my hands."

Earl shivered. "I spent the entire day walking the streets and talking to the business folks along the way. They're scared."

"I know and it's my job to solve this case."

The boisterous kids pushed open the school door and ran down the steps. Earl slid out of the car and waved to get Jack and Tommy's attention. Virgil saw that Susan Welsh stood beside Nelda Morgan who had a girl about Tommy's age.

Jack and Tommy ran to the car. "Hi, Uncle Virgil. Earl, whatcha doing here?"

"Picking you up."

Tommy propped his chin on top of the front seat. "My mom or Uncle Virgil always does that."

"Well, now you got me, too."

Virgil drove away and dropped the boys off at Maggie's. She'd keep them inside unless one of her other boys was busy outside and could keep an eye on them. Virgil decided it was time he drove to St. Louis and have a talk with Dan Martin. Shake him down. Put the fear of God in him. Something so there would be a little peace around the Carter home.

Earl got out and climbed the steps to this house. Virgil admired that the older man cared enough for Jack and Cora to take the time to protect them from harm. No telling when that might come in handy.

He returned to his office, just as Frank was running for the fire truck. Frustration and anger tightened his jaw. "What's burning now?"

"The empty field between the Lucky Lady Mine and the Loosey Goosey."

"Well, for crying out loud. Businesses, the school and now empty fields. What the hell is this guy after? And what happened to our peaceful little town?"

Frank tossed him a hard helmet. "It's about to go up in flames."

CHAPTER SEVENTEEN

Cora arrived at Maggie's to get Jack only to learn Virgil and Frank had been sent out on another fire. "Where?"

Maggie shrugged. "I have no idea. I just heard the sirens and Lester down the street shouting Frank and Virgil were on their way to another fire."

Cora rubbed her forehead. "Honestly, can't we get a break?"

"I'm beginning to wonder just what the heck has brought on all this."

Cora shook her head. "It keeps Virgil up nights. He hasn't rested since the first fire."

"That's too bad." Maggie held out her hand. "But the whole town is depending on Virgil. We don't know where else to turn."

"I understand. It's just such a mystery why a person would torch people's property. It makes no sense."

"I agree."

Cora took Jack home and allowed Tommy to come along and have dinner with them. Since Maggie always watched Jack after school, she felt it only right to return the favor. Inside, the boys shed their coats while Cora put her purse up then went to the bedroom to change into comfortable clothes.

The bed looked inviting. She'd been tired lately and was barely able to keep her eyes open. Yesterday she'd actually taken a nap in one of the rooms during her lunch break.

She checked the icebox trying to decide what to cook but nothing sounded good. Thinking of the males in the house, she fixed chicken and dumplings. That was always a good choice. Also, she turned out the dough she'd left on the counter to rise this morning and put two loaves of bread in the oven to bake.

There was leftover apple pie for dessert and, once again, Cora's thoughts went to Thanksgiving. She had so much to prepare over the next two days. And if these fires didn't stop, Virgil wasn't going to have much of a holiday.

With the boys playing army games in Jack's bedroom, Earl showed up at the back door. "You're early," Cora said. "Supper won't be ready for a while."

"I got plans tonight. I'll be eating over at the Glover's tonight. They asked me on Sunday."

"That's nice of them. I'm sure they're still struggling with Jacob's death."

"Losing a child is always hard, no matter the reason. But, they realize they have to go on living, if for no other reason than the other children they have."

Cora paused in the middle of checking on the chicken and dumplings and looked at Earl who stood near the coffee pot. "Aren't all their children grown?"

"Yes, Jacob was the youngest, but now they're going to be grandparents soon. Prouder than punch."

"Isn't that wonderful?" While Earl poured coffee, Cora thought about her inability to add to her and Virgil's family. But listening to the sound of Jack's laughter reminded her of how lucky she was to have a child to love at all.

He meant everything to her and Virgil.

She cleared her throat and shoved the thought of other children out of her mind. She was the luckiest woman in the world. "So, what have you heard about the fire?"

"Field's on fire. Nothing serious. It appears one of the miners might have been careless with his carbine light on his hat."

"Thank God, at least it wasn't set deliberately."

"I'm not a hundred percent sure, but that's what I hear."

"Maybe Virgil will be home for supper."

"I have to get going. After supper I'm meeting up with Arthur and the judge and we're going to try to come up with a new preacher."

"That's good. The town needs one."

"We figured that. Might as well get on with it."

"I'm sure you'll pick the best person for the job."

"Didn't last time."

"Well, Reverend Fuller is a strange person. No one expected things to happen the way they did."

"Well, I'm off."

Earl left out the back door and Virgil entered through the front. He was covered with black soot. "Hell of a fire."

"Wash up. Supper's almost ready."

He grinned, his white teeth showing up against his blackened face. "Don't you want a kiss first?"

She laughed and stepped back. "I think I can wait."

Hearing the bathroom door close, Cora went back to getting dinner ready. Thoughts of Dr. Adams ran through her head and she worried that she might have a problem on her hands. One that she should maybe discuss with Virgil.

Then again, would a doctor do anything illegal? And what was his motive besides jealousy? Why did he care if she worked there as a doctor? It had nothing to do with his career or anything else.

Virgil came up behind her, making her jump. "You scared me."

"Why?" Taking her by the shoulders, he turned her to face him. "What's wrong?"

She licked her lips. "Nothing."

He dipped his chin. "Don't keep things from me."

She stepped out of his embrace, hoping to distract him. "I'm not. It's silly."

"Let me determine that."

"Dr. Adams let me know what he thought of women doctors today."

"Why does he care?"

She shrugged. "I don't know."

"Has he said anything directly?"

With everything else on his mind, Cora didn't want to worry him unnecessarily. "No, and I'm sure it's just my imagination."

He stepped between her and the stove. Tilting her chin up, he gazed into her eyes. "You look tired."

"I am. I don't know why, but no matter how much I sleep, I feel like I could close my eyes at any given time and doze off."

"Maybe you shouldn't have gone to St. Louis with Thanksgiving so close."

"No, I'm glad I went." She placed her hands on his chest. "I'm taking tomorrow off. I have to get ready for the holiday dinner and Jack's out of school."

"Oh, I almost forgot about going to mom and dad's in a few days."

"Thanksgiving is day after tomorrow."

"Where have the last few months gone? It seems like only yesterday that we got married."

"Who got married?" Jack called out.

Virgil reached over and rustled Jack hair. "Your Aunt Cora and I."

"Oh," the young boy said. "When are we eating, I'm hungry?"

"Me too," Tommy added.

Pal stood between the boys, his tongue out, his tail wagging.

"I'm putting dinner on the table now."

As she and Virgil prepared the table, Jack and Tommy washed up for dinner.

"Earl said the fire was in an empty field."

"Yeah, this time. It looks like it was an accident."

"Anyone hurt?"

Virgil shook his head. "No, we got there pretty quick. The first hint of smoke and the residents are on the phone."

"Good, maybe that will keep someone from getting hurt."

"Well, everyone is on guard, that's for sure."

She took the plates out of his hands and checked his palms. The blisters were mostly gone and the redness had subsided. "Looks like you're healing nicely."

He took the plate from her. "I wasn't hurt to begin with." He scowled. "You pamper me too much."

"Good."

Mumbling, Virgil went about setting the table.

After sitting down, Cora looked at her plate of food and wondered if she'd be able to swallow. Her stomach churned and she fought the urge to get up and run to the bathroom and vomit.

She must have caught a stomach bug or something. Shoving her plate aside, she took a slice of bread and sipped water.

Putting his fork down, Virgil reached over and covered her hand. "You okay?"

"Just not hungry."

He studied her for a few moments then said, "Why don't you take a nap. The boys and I can clean up the kitchen and I'll see that Tommy gets home safely."

She looked at him and forced a smile. "I think I will. My stomach has been acting up for the last few days."

"Maybe you're coming down with something."

"If I am, I hope you and Jack don't get it."

Shoving back her chair, Cora left the kitchen and went to the bedroom. She thought about taking a quick bath, but decided she didn't have the energy. Releasing a tired breath, Cora closed the door and undressed.

CHAPTER EIGHTEEN

Virgil and Jack came back from Maggie's where they'd left Tommy. He'd cleaned the kitchen while the boys listened to their radio program and Pal lay on his back, paws stuck up in the air, snoring between them.

Now, with Jack in bed, Virgil checked in the bedroom to find Cora sound asleep. From the very beginning he'd been against her going to St. Louis. Now, she was exhausted. Damn Clare Williams. If he had his way, the woman would never contact Cora again.

As he went to the kitchen for another cup of coffee, a knock sounded at the door. Carl stood on the other side.

Stepping back, Virgil invited him in. "What's on your mind tonight?"

Carl stomped his booted feet and shook the snow off his shoulders before entering the house. Shoving his gloves in his pockets, he shook his head. "Got a funny feeling, Virgil."

Curious, Virgil asked, "About what?"

"I think that damned Eddie is behind all these fires."

"Why would you think that?"

"I've been watching the filling station at night and I've noticed a few strange things."

"Come in and warm up with a cup of coffee. I was just going to have one."

"Where's your wife and kid?"

"Sleeping."

His war buddy removed his coat and threw it across the back of the couch. After stomping his feet again, he walked across the living room and into the kitchen.

Virgil poured two cups of coffee, shoved the apple pie next to Carl then looked to his friend and said, "Tell me what's on your mind."

Carl sliced a piece of pie and scooped it into a saucer Cora had set out earlier. Virgil decided to have a piece as well.

Licking his finger, Carl said, "Things at Eddie's ain't right."

"Like what?"

"Yesterday he had to have his kerosene tank refilled. Now, I watch that place like a hawk and I don't see too many people buying that stuff from him."

Virgil knew a little about that business from the years he helped out his father. "His tank could've been low from the beginning. The need always rises in the winter."

"Yeah. I agree. The day we opened the Pit Stop we called and they came out to fill up our tank because it was empty. The driver said he was going across the street and top off Eddie's tank."

"How much was that."

"I don't know. But, he carries the same as we do. Fifty-five gallons. He's getting a refill and my tank is over half full."

"I questioned him a few days ago and he claimed he didn't hardly sell much kerosene."

"Then where's it all going?"

Carl brought up a very interesting point. Eddie being behind all the fires made sense if he intended to set the Pit Stop on fire. That would eliminate his competition and put him right back on top. Everyone would believe the Pit Stop was just another victim.

Something else crossed his mind. The gas station owner said he had the money to hold out until his business picked up, but his father had said that Eddie mortgaged his home to get the loan for the business to start with. Had his profits been so high that he was able to pay off the loan and stash back a bunch of money?

Things weren't adding up. Virgil took a bite of the pie and looked at Carl. "If you tell other people that story they'll think you're just trying to place the blame on Eddie."

"That's why I ain't said nothing to nobody. Not even Buford." Carl held up his fork. "But, I've been watching."

"So, he's going through the kerosene and we're not sure about his finances."

"Mind if I have a little more coffee?" Carl asked. "That pie's delicious."

"Sure, help yourself to the pot." He shoved the pie closer. "Enjoy."

Carl passed on the second piece of pie, but sipped the coffee. Virgil thought back to the scenes of the fires, the conversations with the townsfolk and Eddie's familiar face at the citizen's meeting. He'd been all for everyone doing their part.

"Let's keep this quiet for a few days. Give me the name of that kerosene supplier and I'll do some checking." He leaned closer, placing his hand on Carl's forearm. "You know what this means, don't you?"

"Yep, Eddie plans to burn my and Buford's place to the ground. Hopefully, with us inside."

"I wouldn't go that far, but my guess is the Pit Stop is the real target."

Carl relaxed and hooked his elbow over the back of the chair. "I just wanted you to know. I left Archie at the station, I have to get back."

"Good idea."

"I'm spending the nights there and your dad's been keeping a sharp eye out during the day. We'll be careful."

Virgil walked him to the door. "You need a lift?"

Carl slipped on his heavy coat. "Naw, I'll be there before you can warm up the car." He opened the door. "Stay in touch."

"I'll contact you in the next couple of days. Are you going to be open Thanksgiving Day?"

"Yes, we hope to get those traveling to visit families. They'll need a place for gas and a few treats for the kids."

"Be sharp. It's not Eddie doing this personally. My guess is it's one, if not all three, of his boys. They're big and mean. Don't mess with them."

Carl tipped his hat and left, leaving Virgil alone with his thoughts. If Eddie was the culprit, there was no telling when or what he'd hit next. And with the holiday, people would be distracted.

He quickly checked in on Jack and Cora, slipped on his coat and locked the door behind him. He got to his squad car and started the engine. He cruised the streets looking for Ethan. He had to share the information he'd just learned.

He spotted the other squad car outside Betty's Diner. He saw through the big, square window that Ethan sat at the counter sipping a cup of coffee. Except for Ethan, the place was empty.

Leaving the car running, Virgil went inside and took the stool next to his deputy. "Hey, Ethan, how's it going?"

"Pretty good. Everything has been pretty quiet." He looked around. "What are you doing out and about at this time of the night?"

"Carl just left my house. He had a few facts to share that I think you need to be made aware of."

"Shoot."

The waitress came over. "You want coffee, Sheriff Carter?"

"No, I'll only be a minute." He turned back to Ethan. "I want you to keep an eye on Eddie and his sons. Make your presence known. Drive by their home, their filling station and check out the kerosene drum."

"What am I looking for?"

"Nothing really, I just want them to be aware that we're on top of them should they have anything planned while we're all having Thanksgiving dinner."

"Caroline and my sister are preparing food that day. I plan to eat with my family then get back on duty."

"Okay, I won't be too long, either." He stood. "That day I want one of our cars parked in front of Eddie's station."

"I understand."

Virgil patted him on the back. "Good, I'll see you tomorrow."

The next day, Virgil was having his last cup of coffee before leaving for work when Cora came out of the bedroom rubbing her eyes.

"Did you sleep well?"

She walked over and put her arms around his waist and pressed her cheek to his chest. "Very well, after you woke me."

He captured her lips in a deep kiss. "I should've let you sleep, but I couldn't resist."

She smiled slyly. "I glad you didn't."

"You said Jack didn't have school today, so I didn't wake him."

"Good, I'll have a few minutes to myself to get dressed. Today I have to get the turkey and a few things from the store. Your mother's fixing pies and the side dishes, but I'm thinking about a chocolate cake."

"You already have enough to do. Enjoy your day off and catch up on your rest."

Virgil reluctantly tore himself away from his wife and left for work. He drove slowly down Main Street to Broadway and passed Eddie's station. Buford was busy across the street. Virgil waved at his dad, who was selling antifreeze to a customer.

Eddie stood in front of the big window with reduced prices painted all over the glass. He didn't look happy, in fact, when Virgil waved, Eddie turned and disappeared.

At the office, Virgil greeted Ethan as he was leaving for the day. "I stopped by Eddie's several times and made sure he saw me watching his home. Far as I could tell he and two of his sons were home and the oldest stayed at the station last night."

"Good, I'm checking out a few things, but most people are off today. It being this time of year, people aren't as careful as usual."

"We won't take a day off until the person setting those fires is behind bars."

Virgil nodded. "I want to see what I can get done today."

"Good luck. Call and wake me up if you need to."

"I don't want to do that unless I have to. Get some rest."

Ethan left and Virgil went into his office and called Gene McKinnon, only to learn he wouldn't be in his office that day or Thanksgiving Day. He then called the kerosene provider Carl had mentioned but they were closed as well. Frustrated, Virgil stood and walked toward the coffee pot.

Judge Garner came through the door dressed in his casual clothes. "You not working today, either?"

"Court's closed."

"Good for you. I wish I could take some time away from here."

"You can. No one's pushing but you."

Virgil held up the pot, the judge shook his head. Filling his cup, he walked back into his office. "I'm doing what needs to be done because I want this person off the streets of my town."

"We all do."

"Carl came by last night with some interesting things to say." He pointed to the phone. "I can't do much today because Thanksgiving is tomorrow and like you, people aren't working."

"What did Carl say?"

"He's been keeping an eye on Eddie's place and noticed an excessive amount of kerosene being used."

"Could be Carl wants to blame all this on his competition?"

"I told him that's what people would believe."

The judge pulled at his earlobe. "It's what people may say, but they may not believe it. I don't think Carl would make up anything. He likes his liquor, but he's honest."

"So, anyway, I'm going to trying to get to the bottom of what Carl said. If I can get any evidence, I'll arrest Eddie."

"Eddie may be behind this, but he's not setting the fires. If he has anything to do with it, he's probably putting his boys up to it."

"Will you give me a warrant to check Eddie's bank records?"

Judge Garner leaned back and studied him. "Contact the kerosene company first. You find what you suspect, I'll sign the warrant."

Judge Garner left and Virgil wanted to do something besides pace his office. Restless, he left and went to Carl's station just as his father drove up in his old pickup truck.

"I saw you earlier. It's mighty cold for you to be out and about," Virgil said, patting his dad on the back.

"I had to make a run to the hardware store. Besides, I decided to get out of the house and leave your mother to her baking. She comes up with too much for me to do."

"I imagine it's about the same at my house." Virgil looked across the street. Eddie and Son's hadn't even bothered to open up yet. "They always wait this late to serve their customers?"

"Sometimes they don't open until noon."

"Can't keep your business like that."

"That's what I told Carl and Buford. I have to say, they're both here bright and early every morning."

"Good habit to get into. This way people know they can depend on you."

His dad nodded toward the other station. "Yeah, I don't have any idea how he stays open."

Thumbing over his shoulder, Roy walked into the garage. "They don't even seem that concerned about the fires. The other night I came into town and there wasn't anyone there guarding the place."

"Maybe they were taking a snooze."

"Then I don't know who it'd be because Eddie and all three of his sons were at the honky tonk drinking."

Virgil put his hands on his hips. "Now how do you know that?"

"Mervin told me. I saw him at Anderson's hardware store just now and we got to talking and next thing I know the conversation turned to the fires."

"Almost all talk does lately."

"Anyway, I told him I was worried about the gas stations and he said Eddie and his boys weren't because they're out at the honky tonk a couple of nights a week."

That didn't add up. "Eddie told me one of the boys was guarding the station every night."

His father shrugged. "Well, either he's lying or Mervin is. Who's got a reason?"

"I don't know, but we're watching the place."

"Good idea." Inside the station, his father called out. "Mornin' everyone." There were mutters from the garage and Archie walked over and took his coat off the hook and slipped it on. "It's all yours, Mr. Carter."

"Quiet night?"

"Not a thing going on this side of town. Ethan was out and about. Saw him drive by several times."

"Okay, well you go home and get yourself some sleep."

"I'll be back this afternoon unless mom has stuff for me to do. Her sister is coming to town later today and she's been on a cleaning spree."

Virgil chuckled. It felt good to have Carl's family back on track. He went into the bay and called out. Buford raised his head, wiped his hands then smiled. "What brings you around?"

Carl joined them. He had an old starter in his hand. "You or Ethan gonna be working tomorrow?"

"We'll be keeping an eye on things."

"Good," Carl said, "I still got that bad feeling."

CHAPTER NINETEEN

Cora was busy all morning preparing for the big dinner tomorrow at Virgil's parents' house. Jack was visiting Tommy and she planned this afternoon to take them to town with her when she went to the grocery store. This way the boys would get outside, even if it was freezing.

Maybe she'd get them a piece of candy at the store. That always made them happy. As she hummed along, finally feeling better, she noticed a car stopped in front of her house. Thinking it might be Virgil, she walked to the front door only to find a tall, well-dressed man with a briefcase in his hand.

"May I help you?" she asked, unsure what the man wanted.

"You Cora Williams?"

"I'm Cora Carter."

"Either way I have some documents here for you."

She took the papers and studied them carefully. Dan Martin's name jumped out at her, Jack's name appeared everywhere in the text. Uncertain, she looked at the man. "What's this all about?"

"Mr. Martin is suing to render his son back into his custody."

"You must be kidding. Dan doesn't want Jack."

"Nevertheless, he has filed a petition claiming you're unfit and the child should be returned to his father."

She held out the paper. "Are you serious about this? Dan literality gave me the child."

"No, he rendered custody to Robert and Clare Williams. They then gave you custody. That was never Mr. Martin's intent."

Anger boiled up inside her. "Are you not listening to me? No one but me even wanted Jack."

"Even so, the father has the right to ask the courts to reconsider."

Tears filled her eyes and dread squeezed her chest so tightly she could barely breathe. The man on her porch became a blur as tears streamed down her face. "Please," she whispered, "don't take Jack away from me. He's all I have." She clutched the man's coat lapels to keep her knees from buckling. He tried to pry her loose. "The child means everything to me."

"Ma'am, let me go. Mr. Martin is just my client. This isn't my decision."

"No, please, I beg you. I'll do anything he wants. Anything. Just don't take Jack. He's just beginning to thrive and enjoy life. A life I created for him. I can't..."

In the next instant Virgil bounced up the steps and grabbed her around the waist. "What's going on?"

"He's taking Jack."

Finally free of her grasp, the well-dressed man backed up and straightened his suit. "I'm here as Mr. Dan Martin's attorney. He's petitioned for custody of his son, Jack."

Virgil turned on the man. "Get off this property." When the man just stared at him, Virgil stomped his foot. "Get."

"It would all be much easier to just hand over the boy and avoid all this. No child should be dragged through the court system."

"We'll never hand him over to anyone. You tell Dan Martin to bring all he's got, because there's no way in hell he's taking Jack." Virgil shoved the man and he stumbled down the stairs. "Dan Martin will live to regret the day he sent you here to take our boy. You be sure to tell him that."

Obviously scared out of his mind, the man adjusted his hat and ran to his car. Without looking at them, he sped away. Virgil helped her into the house and to the kitchen table where she collapsed into the chair. He took the seat across from her, took the papers from her grasp and held her hand.

Nausea and a burning chill coursed through her entire body. A shiver shook her and her hands trembled. "What are we going to do?"

"Nothing right now." Virgil smoothed the papers out on the table. "We've got time. Don't worry. We'll fight this and we'll win."

"But, he's Jack's father."

Virgil's face twisted. "That man's not a father. He doesn't love Jack. He just wants to hurt you. That's all."

She grasped his hand. "I can't give Jack up. I nearly died when I had to give Ronnie to Susan and Ben. But, Dan will take Jack away. I'll never see him again."

"Now, we don't know that yet."

She noticed even he struggled back tears.

Jack.

Their perfect child. The one they loved so dearly and deeply. How could they go on without him?

Jack would be back to the attic without love or hope. His strong, little spirit would die a slow death and she wouldn't be there to help him. She couldn't save him.

God help her, this was the worst thing that could happen. Even prison didn't hold a candle to this pain. This agony. She couldn't breathe, couldn't think, couldn't feel.

She wanted to curl into a ball and die.

God, no!

Everything blurred as Virgil studied the papers the lawyer had left. Had that stupid man thought that they'd just hand Jack over to him? That they'd roll over and play dead? No, she'd fight to the death to keep Jack.

Dan Martin had to die. She'd kill him. Yes, she had the courage to do that to save Jack. She'd do anything she could imagine to keep his father away from the boy.

In the distance, the phone rang. Virgil answered and came back to sit next to her. "That was Maggie. The boys will be coming over in a few minutes. Do you want me to take them for lunch or something to give you time to compose yourself?"

"No, I want Jack. I need him with me." She turned and grabbed the sleeve of Virgil jacket. "You go get them. I don't want the lawyer to snatch Jack up and drive away with him."

"He's not going to do that. It would be kidnapping." He loosened her hand and smiled. "I'll go get the boys. You wait here."

When he left, emptiness filled the house. Cora tried to swallow but couldn't. Her throat wouldn't cooperate. She tried to stand, but wasn't able to let go of the chair so she sat back down.

Earl came to the back door and after glancing at her briefly, he dropped to his knees beside her. "What's wrong, Missy?" He took her hand. "Why are you crying?"

"Dan's lawyer came by today. He wants Jack. They're going to take my baby away from me."

"The hell they are." Earl stood, put on the coffee to heat and returned to put his hand on her shoulder. "Now don't you worry. These things have a way of working themselves out."

"No, Dan's Jack's father. The real parents always win."

"Not here in Gibbs City, they don't."

"I think it's going to be in St. Louis."

Earl picked up the papers just as the coffee began to perk. He turned and removed the pot from the fire, then went back to reading. "It is up to those courts since that's where the original document was made up."

Tears welled anew. "See, we don't stand a chance."

Virgil came in with the boys and Cora dropped to her knees and grabbed a bewildered Jack in a tight hug. She buried her nose in the young lad's hair and captured his innocent scent. Brushing her hand across his shoulders, she realized that one day he'd grow into a strong, courageous man. He'd graduate high school, go to college, and become a man with his own family. If Dan didn't corrupt him first.

But, she'd never see that. All she'd have would be memories.

Virgil and Earl helped her to a chair.

"What's wrong, Aunt Cora. You look like you seen Casper the Ghost."

Virgil put his hand on Jack's back. "She's a mite upset. You boys go play in your room."

In a flash they were gone, completely unaware that Jack's life might change dramatically by the ruling of the justice system.

Virgil stood over her while Earl poured a cup of coffee, but the smell alone made her sick to her stomach. "I don't want anything."

"What do you make of this, Virgil?" Earl asked. "This guy got a case?"

"I'm taking those to Judge Garner this afternoon. I don't care if it's a holiday or not. We have to get a lawyer. Probably someone in St. Louis."

"We could shoot the bastard," Earl chimed in. "That's the fastest, the cleanest and the easiest."

Virgil pulled out a chair and sat down. "We can't go shooting anyone. It's best we keep that kind of talk quiet. Next thing you know, it'll be repeated and lessen our chances to win this case."

Cora leaned closer. "Do you think we can win this?"

"Why the hell not? You're a good mother. You're a doctor and you've taken care of Jack for the last six months. Where the hell has Dan Martin been? He hasn't even visited or inquired about his own son."

"After my sister died and they took Jack to my parents, I don't think any of the Martins ever went to see him."

Earl harrumphed. "That won't look good to a judge."

"Let me talk to JJ and Francis. They know the law and I'm sure one of them can recommend an attorney."

Wringing her hands, she nodded then closed her eyes. How could she bear this pain? How could she keep calm enough not to upset Jack? She didn't want him to know there was even a remote chance that he'd be taken away from her. It would upset him too much.

Taking a calming breath, Cora got up and washed her face at the kitchen sink. Her nose buried in the towel, she made a promise to herself that she'd act as normal as possible for Jack's sake. She turned to Virgil and Earl. "I'm taking the boys downtown to the grocery. I'll be home in about an hour."

"Do you think you should do that as upset as you are?" Earl asked. "I can run and get whatever you need."

"No," she replied. "The boys need to burn off some energy and they'll want a piece of candy."

Unsteady legs carried her to Jack's room. She put on a smile. "You boys want to go to town with me? I might be tempted, if you're good, to buy you something sweet."

The boys jumped up off the floor with Pal barking behind them. They had their coats on before she could say another word. She buttoned everyone up, took her purse and waved to Virgil and Earl. "We won't be long."

Pal fell in behind them and they walked down the steps toward town as a wave of doubt crushed Cora's heart.

CHAPTER TWENTY

Virgil glanced up at Earl and saw his concern. "We can't let that family continue to tear Cora apart."

"You're right. This nonsense has to stop before Cora has a nervous breakdown." Earl shoved his cup away. "Makes me want to choke Dan Martin to death just to keep him away from Cora and Jack."

"I can understand the way you feel, but killing Dan is out of the question. We'd be the first two they'd look at." Waving the paper, Virgil stood. "I'm going to see the judge."

"He and Ida are going to her family in Joplin for Thanksgiving dinner. They're leaving today."

Slipping on his jacket, Virgil stalked to the door. "Maybe I can catch him before they leave."

He pulled up at the judge's residence and noticed Garner's automobile was still in the driveway. Turning off the engine, he shut the door and approached the house. Judge Garner met him with an open door. "Virgil, come in. We were just leaving."

He handed his friend the papers and waited. Reading them slowly, the judge looked at him and nodded toward his study. "Let's discuss this in private." He glanced at Ida standing with her coat draped over her arm. "We'll be a minute."

The judge waved him inside his study then closed the door. As he moved to the desk, he said. "I have to say, I'm not surprised. I feared it would come to this."

"Why? Dan gave her Jack and hasn't even come around to see how his own son is doing."

"It's not about Jack, it's about the fact that Cora's mother killed his father and ruined his family's name and their business." Francis sat down. "From what I observed at the trial, Dan's mother and Cora's mother hated each other. I think this is more about them than anything."

"You think she put Dan up to this?"

Judge Garner folded his hands on the papers. "I do." He lowered his head. "Those two don't want Jack, they just want to hurt Cora because they can't get to Clare."

Virgil realized that made perfect sense. They were just using Jack to break Cora's heart. "Do you think we can talk sense into them?"

The judge shook his head. "Those people are so eaten up with hatred there'll be no reasoning with them. My guess is they'll fight to the bitter end."

"And poor Jack will probably be ripped from Cora's loving arms and away from the only real family he's ever known." He bit back tears. "I don't think Cora can take that."

"She might not have a choice."

"Is there nothing we can do?"

"Oh, there are plenty of legal moves we can make. I have a friend who can represent Cora in court. He's a damned good lawyer, but we still have to get a judge to take our side of this case."

"Is that possible?"

"Yes, it is. However, I'd like to get the case moved here." He handed the papers back to Virgil and got up to walk around the desk. "Let's meet with JJ on Monday and see what he has to say. After all, this is where Jack lives. She was given permission by the courts in St. Louis to move him here. So there's a possibility that the District Attorney will agree to have the trial moved here."

"Will you be the presiding judge?"

"No, I'll recuse myself, but you stand a better chance here than in St. Louis."

Virgil put his hat on and followed the judge to the door. "Thanks for your time." His tipped his hat at Ida. "Enjoy your holiday, ma'am."

The judge clasped his shoulder. "Have dinner with your family tomorrow and we'll talk after the weekend."

Virgil went out into the swirling snow and trudged his way to the squad car then drove to the station. He hated that Dan's lawyer had delivered the papers today so as to put a damper on their Thanksgiving, but he was sure Dan and his mother planned it that way.

Carl leaned against Virgil's desk twisting a pair of gloves. "What's up?"

His friend looked nervous. "I came to say I'm sorry about this mess with Cora and Jack's dad."

Virgil sat on the edge of Ethan's desk. "My, news travels fast in this town."

"I ran by Betty's Diner to grab lunch for me and Buford. While I was there, I saw Earl and Arthur talking to some young stranger in a suit. When he left, Earl stopped to tell me what was going on."

Virgil shook his head. "Good, old Earl."

"He said he wanted to kill the guy. I know Earl can have a temper, but he looks like he means it this time."

"I'm sure he does, but he shouldn't go spouting his mouth off like that. Next thing I know, I'll have to arrest him."

"He means well, Virgil. Cora and her nephew are the closest things he has to a family."

Virgil let out a sigh. "I know."

"I wanted to drop by and let you know that me, Buford and Archie are going to keep a sharp eye out over the holiday. I'm thinking the person responsible for the fires is looking at this time of year for everyone to be off guard. We won't be."

"Good, that's one less thing on my plate."

"We want you to enjoy your time with your family."

"I'm not taking that much time off. Ethan and I are splitting the day up and taking shifts. If the arsonist thinks we're not on guard maybe they'll make a mistake. Then that will be his downfall."

Carl ducked his head. "I just wanted to come by and tell you that if you need anything, you can count on me."

They shook hands. "I know that, buddy. The whole town does."

Carl left and Virgil thought about the ceremony where everyone in Gibbs City would probably turn out to see Carl get the Outstanding Citizen of the Year award. He'd never been more proud to call Carl friend.

Deciding he needed to make his presence known, Virgil left the office and headed for Main Street. He pushed his way into Glover's market and nodded to Howard. "How's it going?"

"Good, we were able to get things back to normal for the Thanksgiving rush."

"I'm glad to see that."

Eddie came down the aisle to the front of the store. "Hi, Sheriff," he called out, putting the items on the counter. "Getting a few last minute items for the wife."

"That's good." Virgil looked around. "Who's tending the gas station?"

"My oldest."

"Be sure to keep a sharp eye out."

"I'm not worried. My son can handle himself."

"Just be careful. You open tomorrow?"

"No, I'm spending the day with my family."

"Okay, that's good to know. Ethan and I will be out and about all day."

Eddie looked at him with surprise. "You're not having dinner at your parents' tomorrow?"

"I will be there briefly. But, while I'm there I have six men who've volunteered to walk the streets to keep the town safe."

"Really?" Eddie reached for his wallet. "I guess you can never be too careful."

Virgil leaned against the wall and stared hard. "I've asked them to be armed."

Surprise widened Eddie's eyes. "What?"

"They see someone running from a building, I've given them orders to shoot."

"I didn't hear anything about that. Could be dangerous."

"Special ruling by the judge. We have to catch whoever's doing this before someone is burned alive."

Eddie took his sack and stalked out the door. Virgil looked at Howard.

"He appeared a little upset."

Howard watched the door. "I don't think he likes the fact that those men will be armed."

"They won't be, but he doesn't need to know that."

Howard leaned over and stared at the station owner's back. "You suspect Eddie?"

Virgil shrugged. "I'm just protecting my county."

He touched the brim of his hat and left for home. Several men had given up their time and agreed to keep an eye on the streets today. They were all men he felt could be counted on.

Inside the house, Cora was busy cooking and Ronnie had joined the boys playing on the living room rug. Pal contentedly lay beside Jack, his tail wiggling out of control.

Stepping around them, Virgil went to the kitchen. He put his arms around Cora and enfolded her against his body. She was warm and firm with her backside against his crotch. Breathing in her fragrance, he nibbled her neck.

"I talked to the judge," he whispered. "We're meeting with him and JJ on Monday. Try not to worry."

"I can't help it."

"I know, but we have time. Nothing's going to happen right away. The law is slow and that will work to our advantage."

She rubbed her face. "I don't even understand why Dan's doing this."

"The judge thinks it's more his mother than him."

She stilled. "Mrs. Martin? She can't stand her grandson."

"That doesn't mean she doesn't want to hurt you or your mother."

"It all comes back to all the wrongs done in the past. I swear I'm sick of it all."

"I know. I am too. But, I think we have a better chance of keeping Jack than they stand of getting him back."

She turned in his arms and wrapped her arms around his neck. "Why?"

"Well, they gave him away. Don't you think a judge would wonder why the change of heart? And if they gave him away once, would they do it again?"

She nibbled her bottom lip. "That does make sense."

"See, all is not lost. We still have a dog in this fight."

"I'm an ex-con."

"An ex-con who's record has been completely cleared." He kissed her nose. "I filed that paperwork two weeks ago. They can't use that."

Taking a shaky breath she stepped back and sat at the kitchen table. "That makes me feel a little better."

He followed her. "Don't worry yourself sick. You've been working too hard lately. Maybe the three of us need to get away for a day or two."

She reached out and stroked his cheek lovingly. "You won't be able to do anything until you arrest the person responsible for setting those fires." She smiled weakly. "We both know that."

"Yeah, well, maybe that won't be long now."

"Do you have a suspect?"

"I've got my eye on someone."

Earl knocked on the door then entered. He headed straight for the coffee pot. "It's cold out there. I'm ready for summer."

"That's a long ways off, Earl. It's not even Christmas yet."

"I know, but this cold weather makes my poor old bones ache."

With a steaming cup of coffee, Earl took a seat at the table and looked around. "You ain't got anything baked yet?"

Cora rolled her eyes and got back up to retrieve a plate of cookies from the kitchen counter. "I'm only making a chocolate cake for dessert. Minnie is doing pumpkin pies."

Earl took a cookie, holding it in the air. "Now that woman can bake those kinds of pies. Wanda never could get her recipe and never could beat her at the State Fair."

"Mom's the queen in that category. I watched her win dozens of first place ribbons."

"We all did. I never minded because she always slipped me a piece when Wanda wasn't watching. God, how I love pumpkin pie."

"You'll get your share tomorrow."

"I reckon I will. I'm looking forward to the whole meal."

Virgil leaned toward Earl. "Carl said he saw you earlier today at Betty's Diner. Thought you hated the place."

"I do. That woman should be arrested for her cooking. It was only business and all I had was a cup of coffee."

Virgil wondered. "What kind of business are you up to?"

"Me and Arthur met a young fella there who's going to be our preacher. He's a good man, loves the Lord and is from Carthage."

Cora's eyes lit up. "We're getting a new minister?"

"Yes, Daniel Washburn. He's a mighty fine man and came highly recommended."

Virgil stood and poured him and Cora a cup of coffee. "When does he start?"

"The week after this coming Sunday. He'll be saying goodbye to his congregation Sunday, then moving down next week."

"That's good news," Cora said, pushing her coffee aside. "I'm sure you and Arthur made an excellent choice."

"I sure the hell hope so after Fuller. If I ever wanted to bust a man in the chops, it was him."

Virgil tasted his coffee. "The town needs a man of God with all these fires. Hopefully, he'll be a comfort to those in need."

"I have to say, I liked him a lot and so did Arthur." Earl took another cookie. "You find that fire starting fool, yet?"

"I wish, but I think I might be getting closer."

"Good, that person belongs behind bars." Earl looked worried. "Is the town covered during the holiday weekend? Be a perfect time to try something sneaky."

"I have the whole town on alert and several volunteers will be patrolling the streets looking for anything suspicious."

"Good," Earl said. "Hope you catch the no-account sidewinder." He lifted his nose and sniffed. "My, that turkey smells good."

Cora laughed. "It's only been in the over an hour."

"Still makes my mouth water."

Virgil looked at the elderly man and grinned. "What doesn't make your mouth water?"

He looked at Virgil. "You." Pushing himself up, he walked slowly to the coat hooks and retrieved his battered hat and slipped on his coat. At the back door, he said. "Have a great Thanksgiving tomorrow."

They waved goodbye and Maggie came in right behind Earl. "I came to relieve you of Tommy."

Cora stood. "He's no bother at all." She pointed to the three boys. "Ronnie joined them a little while ago and they've been content ever since."

Maggie looked at the youngsters and grinned. "They are the three little musketeers, aren't they?"

"They're very special." Cora looked away. "I hope it stays that way."

Maggie dropped into a chair. "Why, what's wrong."

Cora fought back tears. Setting the cookies on the side table, she rested a hip on the arm of Maggie's chair.

Virgil came up behind her and put his arms around her. "Dan wants to try and get custody of Jack."

"Why that lowlife." Maggie tightened her mouth. "Just shoot him, Virgil. Kill the bastard and put him out of his misery."

"I can't do that. But I'd sure like to."

Maggie clasped Cora's hand. "What are you going to do?"

Cora looked up and that lost expression in her eyes broke his heart. "We'll fight with everything we have."

Maggie's eyes glistened with tear. "God knows, we don't have much, but if there's anything we can do to help, you only have to ask."

Cora managed a smile. "I know I can depend on you."

"Well, if you're okay with Tommy staying here a little longer, I'm going to run to Glover's to pick up a few things. I won't be long."

"Take your time, they've had lunch and I'm just getting ready to offer them milk and cookies."

Maggie gripped Cora's shoulder. "You're the best mother I know."

CHAPTER TWENTY-ONE

Cora fought against the knot in her stomach and the pain in her heart as they loaded up the car and prepared to go to Virgil's parents' house for the big dinner.

On the way Virgil drove so slowly through town she feared the food would get cold before arriving at their destination. Once there, his father, Roy, ran out to greet them and fetch an arm full of food. Jack carried the rolls and darted into the house.

Virgil gave her a tight squeeze before they entered to inhale the wonderful aromas of a Thanksgiving feast. The table was already piled high with the traditional offerings. The turkey took the center space and was cooked to a nice golden brown. Cora was quite proud that the first bird she'd ever baked looked so delicious.

For a brief moment her thoughts traveled to her mother. She'd have no feast today. This would simply be another day behind bars. Cora knew that hurtful feeling and understood there wasn't anything she could do about the situation.

Minnie hugged her and Jack then stood back to admire the table. "My, that's enough food to make any family proud." She looked to Virgil's father. "Roy, go get the Brownie camera and take some pictures. We all need to remember our first holiday together as a family."

After several clicks and flashes, they were seated and Jack asked for a drumstick. When Virgil carved the turkey and handed him one, the boy's eyes nearly popped out of his head. "Gosh, that's big."

Virgil grinned. "You think you can handle it?"

"I'm sure gonna try."

Cora's appetite continued to be off but she chalked it up to nerves about the possibility of losing Jack. She immediately put those thoughts aside. She refused to ruin their first Thanksgiving together. She'd have plenty of time to worry about what the future held.

As Cora passed Virgil's dad the sweet potatoes and Minnie picked up the gravy dish, she smiled at the prospect of having a real, loving family. Virgil's parents had accepted her and Jack without reservations. They were kind, gracious and wanted to be grandparents to Jack. Virgil's dad and Jack were always cooking up something.

Earlier, while she and Minnie laid out the food, Virgil and Roy took Jack behind the house to play with an old sled found in the attic. The boy's squeals filled the air and had them all laughing.

Now that they were enjoying the meal, Cora decided not to mention anything about the possibility of losing her nephew. No need to worry them because right now was such a happy time.

"I'll sure be glad when you arrest the fool setting those fires," Minnie said.

"That would be a relief. Do it before anyone else gets hurt," Roy agreed.

"I'm trying. We're watching practically everyone in town."

"If they were smart they'd burn down Betty's Diner. The food she serves should be against the law."

Cora dabbed her lips. "Earl agrees, I believe. But it's too bad for the single miners who have no place else to eat."

Roy put down his fork and raised his glass of iced tea. "They can eat their fill at the main houses."

Cora hadn't heard that before. "What is a main house?"

"Every mine has what's called a main house where the single miners sleep and eat. The mine owners just deduct it from their wages."

Cora thought for a few seconds. "Why haven't I ever seen one before?"

Minnie looked at her. "They're all on the outside of town where the mines are."

"I thought those were just offices or something like that."

Roy shook his head. "No, all mining business is conducted in town. Those buildings are for the miners."

"What's a miner," Jack asked.

Roy leaned down. "Not something you ever want to be. Mining is dangerous work. Best to stay above ground. It's healthier."

They finished the meal and Minnie brought out fresh coffee to go with her pumpkin pie and Cora's chocolate cake. Virgil and his dad had a piece of each. Jack went right for the cake.

How thankful she was to be here, in this house, with these people. They were truly her family. She could depend on them and they let her know it.

Cora had always loved coffee, but lately she could barely stand the smell of it. When she turned down a cup, Minnie offered her a warm cup of tea and she accepted. It tasted delicious.

She was so full, she didn't think she could budge, but when the three of them decided to teach her pinochle, Cora couldn't resist. Jack had a new coloring book and crayons Minnie had produced to keep him occupied. In the end, Virgil and his father won the card game, but they'd all had a good time.

After cleaning the dishes and the kitchen, they left for home with a car full of leftovers. On the way back, Virgil detoured down several streets before arriving at the house. It wasn't dark yet, but Jack was half asleep when Virgil carried him inside. Cora had an arm load of food when Ethan pulled up and honked. She turned, held up a bowl and smiled. "You hungry?"

"No, thank you. I'm still about to bust from earlier. But I am looking for Virgil."

Just then Virgil came outside and walked to the car. "What's up?"

"Just wanted to let you know that there was a small fire over by the courthouse. Frank didn't think it was our arsonist, but I figured you should know."

"Thanks for coming by."

Cora leaned down and looked through the side window of the squad car. "Anyone hurt?"

"Nope, I think it was just a couple of kids playing around."

"I hope you're right." Cora went into the house and set the food on the table. Removing her coat, she put things away and asked Jack if he wanted anything.

He seemed content to lie on the couch and scratch Pal's belly. After a few minutes, Virgil came in and hugged her tightly.

"Everything okay?" she asked.

"Yeah, I'm just going to do a quick drive through town. I won't be long."

He left and Cora joined Jack on the couch. "You look tired."

"I had a lot of fun with Grandpa Roy today. He's fun."

"Grandparents always are."

"Can we go there more often?"

"Sure, I don't think Virgil would argue with that."

Feeling lazy and content to put her feet up, Cora fought against the queasiness that had her breathing slowly through her mouth to keep from rushing to the bathroom. She wondered what she'd eaten today that didn't agree with her. If she didn't get better she'd get something from the pharmacy to help settle her stomach.

Virgil came home a couple of hours later and sat on the couch with her. Jack sprawled across both their laps. "You know what?" Virgil asked.

"No, what?"

"I kept thinking how grateful I was today to have you and Jack."

"I felt the same way."

Virgil smiled at Jack. "This is all I need to be happy."

"Good," she laughed. "Because this is all you're getting."

Virgil started tickling her and soon her stomach settled down to normal. A special program came on the radio and Jack was suddenly distracted and excited that Superman was flying through the air.

Virgil laughed. "A man flying. What will they come up with next?"

"Who knows?"

They left the couch and went into the bedroom and lay across the bed. She felt tired and sleepy enough to take a nap, but it was too late in the day to do that and still be able to rest comfortably tonight.

"I really enjoyed having dinner today with your parents. They're wonderful people."

"Yes, they are. I have a lot of memories in that house."

"I bet you miss your brothers."

"Yeah, especially on holidays. I always think this is one family gathering they won't be attending."

She cupped his face with her hands. Pulling him closer, she captured his lips. "I'm so sorry."

"I know," he smiled faintly. "The war changed everything."

"It took a lot of lives."

Virgil looked into the distance. "Sometimes I think the war took the best and we poor bastards left are just a hollow excuse to continue on."

Cora sat up. "You shouldn't say that. Jack and I love you very much." She tilted his chin until their eyes met. "Where would I be without you?" She scowled deeply. "And don't you dare say better off."

They were just relaxing back when there was a loud ruckus on the porch. Men shouted and feet and scuffling carried into the house.

Jack ran into their bedroom and jumped into her arms. Virgil motioned for them to stay in the bedroom and not move. He moved silently to the kitchen, removed his gun from atop the fridge then crept toward to the door.

Cora made Jack stay on the bed with a squirming Pal while she peeked around the doorway. Virgil yanked open the door and staggered back against the doorframe. His arm flew up and the gun slid across the floor.

Before she knew what was happening, a big man tackled Virgil to the floor, but Virgil soon got the upper hand and knocked the man upside the head. Pal had escaped and was biting the legs of the intruder's pants.

Diving for his gun, Virgil came to his feet. "What the hell's going on here?"

Carl and Buford staggered in, black eyes and bloody lips. Carl held on to the doorframe for support. "We found the son of a bitch who's been setting those fires."

CHAPTER TWENTY-TWO

Virgil glanced at Cora and Jack as she hugged the door and Jack gripped her dress. "You two stay inside and don't answer the door."

"What's wrong, Uncle Virgil?"

"Nothing, son. Take Aunt Cora back in the bedroom and stay with her. Keep Pal with you."

Virgil shoved everyone out onto the porch. Dusk was settling in. "What the hell is going on?"

Carl had Eddie's oldest son, Matthew, by the collar. "We saw him running behind the dry cleaners and we followed him. He had a can of kerosene hidden in the old school warehouse."

Buford's breath came in white billows. "We followed him real close. Then he came up behind our place and started dumping the can. That's when we nabbed him."

Virgil looked at the sullen twenty-one year old who stood over six feet tall and pushed the scales at over two hundred pounds. "Let's get everyone to the station." Virgil took Matthew by the arm and went to his cruiser where he took a pair of handcuffs from the side pocket on the door.

"You gonna lock him up, Virgil?" Carl asked.

Slapping the cuffs on Matthew, Virgil looked at Buford and Carl. "Meet me at the station and we'll get this straightened out."

Virgil stopped and looked at Carl. His heart was racing. "Is there anyone at your station now?"

"No, we gave Archie the night off."

Virgil looked at Buford. "You run back to the garage and stay there."

Carl pointed to Matthew. "But we caught him red-handed."

"If he poured out the kerosene, all someone has to do is strike a match and your business is gone." He shook Matthew. "Also Eddie has two more sons. If one's in on it, they all are."

Buford's eyes widened. "I'll get there as soon as I can."

"No, Buford, jump in my truck and I'll drive you," Carl said as both men flew into action.

Virgil didn't have a coat on and he shivered waiting for the heater in the car to kick in. He felt like he'd been on a five mile run with a fifty pound pack on his back. His senses were telling him there would be more trouble. Gritting his teeth, he hoped to God Matthew was working alone and it would be all over with.

"They're liars, Sheriff. I was just out walking off Thanksgiving dinner."

"We'll see. I'm not making any judgments until I hear all the facts."

At the station, Ethan must've heard him pull up because he opened the door and looked confused. "Virgil, what are you doing here?"

He opened the back door to pull Matthew from the seat. When he resisted, Ethan took one elbow and Virgil the other. Inside the station, Ethan emptied his pockets then they both lead him to the jail. Pushing the struggling man into the cell, Virgil slammed the door and locked it with a satisfying bang.

Ethan stood back with his hands on his hips. "What's he doing here?"

"Carl and Buford brought him to my house. They claim he's the one setting the fires. They saw him with kerosene behind their station."

Matthew spit out, "That's a bald-face lie."

Ethan walked toward the cell. "We'll let the facts determine that. But, I can smell the oil from here. You must've gotten some on your clothes. And you had matches on you, but no cigarettes"

"That's gasoline. I work in a filling station."

Ethan pointed his finger at the suspect. "You were closed today. You weren't pumping any gas."

Virgil called Ethan to the side where Matthew couldn't hear them. "I need you to go to the Pit Stop. See if you smell the fumes and can find the can. That will help. We can have Gene run the fingerprints."

"I won't be long."

Ethan left and Virgil put on a fresh pot of coffee. He waited for Carl to come to the station and write out everything he saw. There would be a trial and he wanted to make sure the person responsible for all the damages done to Gibbs City was convicted and put behind bars where he belonged.

The only problem was, Matthew probably was only doing what his daddy put him up to and Eddie wasn't man enough to do the right thing and admit the crime. No, he'd rather let his son sit in jail than him. Virgil hoped somehow he could connect Eddie to the crimes.

Dejected, Matthew sat on the cot in the cell, his head lowered, his hands hanging between his knees. If he thought for one minute his daddy would get him out of this mess, he was mistaken. Virgil almost felt sorry of the young man.

Expecting Carl, Virgil was surprised when Eddie came through the door screaming his fool head off. "Get my son out of that cell right now." He pointed to Virgil. "I'll have your badge. You got no right."

Virgil held out his hands. "Settle down, Eddie. Your boy was caught with a can of kerosene behind the Pit Stop earlier. With all the fires there's cause to suspect Matthew of setting those fires."

"He didn't do anything. Just went for a walk. That's all. Can't a man leave his house without being accused of being a criminal? You just want to blame somebody because your job's on the line. The whole town is threatening to take your badge if you don't find the person setting those fires."

"I haven't heard that, Eddie. Not a single person has expressed that to me or Judge Garner or the Mayor."

"I heard them with my own ears and now you're trying to ruin my son's life."

"I think you've already done a good job of that."

"What are you saying?" Eddie staggered backwards holding his chest. "You think I'm behind this?"

"I do and I've been watching you for some time."

"You're crazy sick in the head. You just go around blaming anyone for everything."

"No, I'm blaming you for putting your boys up to setting those fires."

Ethan and Carl walked in surprised to see Eddie. "What are they doing here?"

"Ethan is the deputy and on duty." He pointed to his friend Carl. "He caught your son trying to burn down his business."

Eddie chuckled loudly. "Why he ain't nothing but the town drunk. Who you think's going to believe him?"

Virgil braced his feet. "I do."

With a rag wrapped around the wooden handle of the gas can, Ethan propped it on his desk. "This is the evidence I found at the scene. Also, there were indications of where someone had splashed a fire accelerant on the back of the building."

"That don't mean it was my son."

Carl stepped forward and tapped Eddie on the chest. "Me and Buford watched him with our own eyes. We seen him sneaking around, making sure no one was looking." Carl tapped Eddie on the chest. "Well, we were."

"Ain't nobody going to believe you."

Virgil stared at Eddie. "The boy stays in jail until Monday when I talk to Judge Garner. If anything happens at the Pit Stop, I'm holding you personally responsible. Now go home."

Eddie's son called out in a tearful voice. "You mean I have to stay here for days."

Eddie quickly ran to the cell and gripped the bars. "Don't worry one bit, Matthew. I'll get you out of here in no time."

"But, I don't want to be here at all."

"Hush and I'll take care of everything."

"Visiting hours are over," Ethan said. "Time for you to leave."

When Eddie reluctantly left, Virgil poured a cup of coffee and had Carl and Ethan joined him in his office with the door closed. Ethan leaned against the wall while Carl took a chair and scooted it closer to his desk.

"We have to be very careful here. I want both of you to write down everything with all the details listed. When I speak to the judge I want to make sure we have an ironclad case."

"I think his father put the boy up to it," Ethan said.

Virgil leaned back in his chair. "I wouldn't be a bit surprised to learn that they're all in on it. But, Matthew may be the one that goes to jail."

"His other sons are too young. The middle boy is a year or two older than Archie, his youngest is maybe fifteen. They aren't old enough to be locked up."

"Yes, they are. And they're old enough to be drinking at a honky tonk. Besides, there are places that will even convict a younger boy if his crime is big enough," Virgil added. "But, in my opinion, Eddie Summerfield needs to be the one sitting in that cell and the one on trial."

"We can probably get Matthew to turn on his daddy."

"I'm sure you're right, but we need proof. If my guess is right, the old man didn't do a bit of the dirty work."

"That son of a bitch," Carl spit. "It ain't right that a parent sets up his own kids."

"You're right," Virgil said after taking a sip of his coffee. "But that's probably the case here."

Carl lowered his head. "I hate to ruin that boy's life."

"You aren't responsible for the consequences of his actions. Let's all go about our business and let Judge Garner settle this. He's out of town and won't be back into his office until

Monday. In the meantime, let's keep the Summerfield kid locked up and we'll see if Eddie is man enough to do the right thing."

Carl jumped to his feet. "You and I know he ain't. He's a greedy old bastard that doesn't care what happens as long as his ass isn't behind bars."

"Just be careful, Carl. I think Eddie had his eye on your place all along. Now we're in a dangerous situation."

Carl scratched his head. "What do you mean?"

Ethan pushed away from the wall and stood next to the desk. "While Matthew is locked up would be the perfect time to set another fire. That would lead people to believe Matthew didn't do it. Someone else had to be setting those fires. If your gas station went up in flames, then Eddie would benefit from your business and that would prove his son is innocent."

Carl nodded slowly. "Oh, I get it. He's killing two birds with one stone."

Virgil looked at his friend. "You and Buford need to be extra careful now. Eddie is going to come after your place and you're going to have to be ready."

Carl gritted his teeth. "I'll catch him in the act. Then we can put his ass behind bars."

"Just stay diligent. I don't want more people hurt. And take care of those cuts."

The men broke up, leaving Ethan to guard the prisoner. Carl headed back to the station and Virgil went on his way to let Cora know he was all right.

He pulled in front of the house and looked at the light streaming from the two front windows. Nothing warmed his heart more than coming home to Cora and Jack. The love he felt for the house, those inside and all around, made Virgil a happy man. Meeting Cora was the best thing that ever happened to him. Yes, Dan wanted to ruin his family, but he wouldn't let that happen.

Freezing, Virgil exited the car and went into the house. Inside, the warmth surrounded him and made his heart beat faster.

Cora looked up from where she stood at the stove. "What happened?"

Taking her face in his cold hands, he kissed her thoroughly and held her close for a moment. Squeezing her briefly, he stepped back to the table and sat down. "I arrested Matthew Summerfield for setting the fires."

"Did he do it?"

"I think his father put him up to it."

Cora's eyes widened. "That's horrible. What kind of parent would do that?"

"The wrong kind."

She put a plate of leftovers in front of him. "I suspect since we ate so early you're hungry."

"Did you eat already?"

"I'm not really hungry."

"Still fighting that stomach trouble?"

She rubbed her belly. "I must've picked up something at the hospital. I'm not running a fever and no aches or pains. All I want to do is sleep."

"Why don't you go take a nap?"

She looked at him and let out a breath and lowered her shoulders. "That's all I've done and I'm still tired."

"You might have one of the doctors check you out Monday."

"I'll stop by the pharmacy and get something."

"I just hope it isn't serious. It's been a rough week for you. Maybe it's all the stress. I promise you we'll get through this."

Her shoulder slumped. "I pray you're right."

"How's Jack?"

"I've finally got him calmed down. He's been anxious ever since you left. He's in his room with Pal on guard. Why don't you go in and let him know you're home. I'll tuck him in in a few minutes. Your dad wore him out on that sled today. I'm glad they're so kind to him."

"As far as they're concerned, Jack's their grandchild."

168

"Well, we all had a lovely day."

"It was fun." So different from last year when his parents were still under the impression he didn't want to come home from the war. They'd been so stiff and cold he couldn't wait to get away. Today he enjoyed lingering over dessert and playing cards.

Virgil finished his meal and went into Jack's room. He sat on the bed to cuddle him and reassure him that the bad guys weren't coming back. He managed to get a smile for the boy and tickled him until Cora came in and together they tucked Jack safely into bed for the night.

Cora disappeared into the bedroom. Maybe once Jack was asleep, he and Cora could relax and unwind. It had been a busy day. Now with Matthew in jail, he hoped the whole fire incidents were over and everyone could be back to living normal lives instead of being afraid to go to sleep at night.

Virgil got up from the sofa and walked into the bedroom. Leaning against the door jamb, he watched as Cora bent down and kissed Jack on the cheek and squeezed his little body tightly against hers. She'd be devastated if Dan took the boy away.

She looked at Virgil and smiled before coming to her feet and turning out the light.

"Goodnight, Jack. Sleep tight," Virgil said.

He and Jack had come to an understanding. Since they were both guys there would be no more kissing between them because they were too manly. But, poor Aunt Cora couldn't help herself, so he'd keep kissing her until she got older.

Virgil smiled. That had been a strange conversation. The boy was growing up before his eyes and there was no way to stop it or slow him down. Before long he'd be more independent and Virgil didn't think his aunt would like that.

Cora left Jack's room and walked into his open arms. He inhaled the scent of her clean hair and mild perfume. He was so glad to have her in his life and he hoped their love for each other grew as the years went by.

The phone rang. Virgil groaned and Cora stepped back with a resigned look. His chest constricted as he lifted the receiver. "Hello."

"Sheriff you better get here fast," Buford's panicked voice echoed the phone line.

"What's happening?"

"Eddie tried to burn down the station and Carl's gone after him with a shotgun."

Grabbing his coat, Virgil ran toward his squad car.

The sound of sirens screamed through the night as he sped toward downtown. Turning into the gas station, Virgil slowed and took out his search light. No sign of Carl or Eddie.

Shouts ricocheted in the distance. He spun the car around and drove down Broadway. He saw the two men. Eddie leading the way with Carl trailing behind him. Virgil, backed up, darted around Main Street and came down the alley.

He jumped from the car, protected by the open door as Eddie ran toward him. "Stop or I'll shoot."

Eddie had a small pistol in his hand and turned back to see Carl closing in on him.

"Put the weapon down and get on the ground."

Eddie pulled the trigger, the bullet missed Carl, but Virgil couldn't take the chance the next one wouldn't. Aiming carefully, he squeezed off a round and Eddie crumpled to the ground.

Virgil quickly ran to the injured man and removed the weapon.

CHAPTER TWENTY-THREE

Cora ran to Earl's and asked him to sit with Jack while she went to see if she could help. She hurried on the slippery sidewalk until she saw Virgil's car then she broke into a run.

She stopped when she noticed a light coming from behind the dry cleaners. Men were standing over a figure lying on the ground. She rushed over and knelt down beside Eddie. He'd been shot in the leg, but the wound was serious enough to be bleeding heavily. Before he died from blood loss, she grabbed a rag from Carl's pocket and tied it tightly in hopes of curtailing the blood flow.

"What happened?"

Carl stepped forward. "I saw a light and when I checked it out, Eddie was back behind the Pit Stop with that book of matches." He pointed to a half empty book of matches. "I told him to stop. When he took off running I could hardly see him." Carl looked at Virgil. "The sheriff shot him in the leg."

The ambulance pulled up, but by that time, the wound barely oozed. They loaded the groaning patient onto a stretcher and took him to the hospital. The emergency room doctor would attend to his injury.

Virgil pulled her close. "What are you doing out in this cold air?"

"I wanted to help." She looked at Carl. "If the bleeding hadn't been stopped he could've died."

Carl looked at his shotgun. "I'm not sure I would've aimed. Probably wouldn't hit anything because my hand was shaking so badly. I just wanted to hold him up until Virgil showed."

"Okay," Virgil said. "Explain how you found Eddie again?"

"Me and Buford were both standing watch. I'd just made a pot of coffee and called him inside when I heard a noise coming from the back of the building."

Carl continued. "I whispered to Buford, and we crept around to the side and that's when I saw Eddie strike the match."

Cora looked around. "Be glad the building didn't go up in flames."

"It probably would've if I hadn't gone home, got my wheelbarrow and loaded it up." Buford shined his flashlight toward the gas station. "I shoveled over where Matthew had poured out the kerosene. Then I washed it from the back of the building. After I dumped fresh dirt and snow on the area, there wasn't anything to catch on fire."

"That was smart thinking, Buford," Carl said, patting his partner on the back. "He sure came to burn us down."

"You both should be happy Eddie didn't kill one of you. He might've shot both of you." Virgil released Cora and planted his hands on his hips. "I'm glad you called, Buford." He looked at his friend. "I'm thankful you didn't have to shoot Eddie. I know that would've been hard on you."

"It all happened the way the Good Lord meant," Buford said.

Virgil ran his hand through his hair. "Okay, I think it's safe to go home for the night. Try to get some sleep and we'll figure everything out on Monday."

He took Cora by the arm and walked toward the car. "Don't come chasing after trouble, young lady." He looked at her sternly. "There was a gun involved. Eddie could've tried to hurt you."

"Yes, but Eddie was bleeding to death. If I hadn't got here when I did, you might've killed a man."

"I make those decisions every day."

"Well, Jack's going to be happy you shot a bad guy."

Virgil chuckled. "If there's a bright side to this, that's it."

On Monday morning, Cora went to work after dealing with nausea and vomiting most of the weekend. She found Stan and told him she thought she might have caught something and asked if he'd heard of anyone else getting sick.

"Are you sure you're not pregnant?"

Cora froze then shook her head slowly. She was a doctor. There was little evidence she was pregnant and after the butcher preformed the last abortion on her, he'd had to remove most of her womb. That left no chance at all for her to become pregnant.

"I know that's not possible, Stan. I had surgery when I was younger. I can't have children."

"I'm sorry to hear that, Cora. But I suggest you talk to Dr. Richie. He's in general practice, but he's also the best Internist we have."

"I'll see if I can make an appointment."

"Try soda crackers until then."

"I wasn't able to keep much down over the weekend."

"I'll have my nurse call and set up an appointment."

Cora went about her day until just before noon when she learned the doctor could see her around two. Feeling better, she was tempted to cancel, but she didn't want Virgil and Jack to catch something from her. Besides, her lunch hadn't stayed down and she could barely keep her eyes open.

She took her coat and purse and left work early. She'd stop by the doctor's, pick up a few things from the grocery then be home in time to pick Jack up from school and cook a nice dinner.

Doctor Hyman Richie's office was clean, neat and there were only two patients ahead of her. When Cora went back, the nurse suggested she undress. Knowing the whole process was unnecessary, Cora thought about arguing, but decided it wasn't worth the energy.

Wearing the cloth gown that she felt barely covered her, Dr. Richie came in. He was a tall man with a head of thick, gray hair and a pudgy face. His kind eyes were filled with compassion and intelligence.

"So, I see by the chart," he began, "that you've been having nausea, feeling tired and certain smells aggravate the situation."

"That's all true, Dr. Richie, but I'm not pregnant. I'm sure you've heard I was in prison."

He nodded, listening carefully.

"While there, three abortions were performed on me. The last one probably left me sterile. I nearly bled to death."

"I understand," he said putting the file down. "Let's take a look and see what we find. Is that okay with you?"

"Yes, but mostly I'd like this nausea to go away."

"Let's see if we can't find the cause."

He checked her thoroughly and when his examination was done, the nurse took blood and a urine samples. Dressed, Cora waited in his office amid stacks of files, medical journals and a small display of older medical instruments.

The door opened and she turned to see the kindly man enter and step behind his desk. Glancing over his notes, he looked up at her and smiled gently. "I didn't find anything unusual. We'll wait and see what the tests reveal. In the meantime, eat light, don't cook anything that upsets your stomach and get lots of rest." He stood. "I'll contact you in a few days."

"Thank you."

Cora left with a sense that nothing had been accomplished. Even now her stomach wouldn't settle down, making her miserable. She stopped at Glover's Market and picked up a few items. They still had plenty of turkey, but by now they were all sick of it.

Carrying a sack home, she wondered if there was the remotest of possibilities she could be pregnant. In prison, they'd given the inmates medicine to stop their monthly times so they could prostitute them any time they wished. Since then, she'd never been regular. But surely after all the abortions and scrapings, there was no way she could conceive.

She hadn't for the last two years and Warden Becker made sure there were plenty of opportunities. No, she was sure this was a bug and eventually she'd be back to normal. However, she didn't buy bacon during her trip to the store. The smell would send her running to the bathroom.

Jack and Virgil came in dusting snow off their coats as she stood in the kitchen preparing dinner. "Did everyone have a nice day?"

While Jack smiled and rubbed Pal's tummy, Virgil came over and pulled her into his arms. "Are you feeling better?"

She kissed him on the lips then smiled. "I went to the doctor and he couldn't find anything wrong, so I'm going to eat a light diet for a few days and see if it all clears up."

"Did you tell him you were always tired?"

"I did and he gave me iron pills to improve my blood."

He released her to help finish dinner, yet he was mostly in her way. In a matter of minutes, Earl came through the door and sat at the table.

As they began eating, Earl asked, "So, what's the verdict on Eddie Summerfield?"

"Ethan took him and Matthew to Carthage today. They were declined bail because Judge Garner thought they were too great a flight risk."

"You don't say."

"I'm glad it's all over," Cora said, shoving her plate aside.

Earl tapped her dish. "You've been off your feed lately. You sick?"

Cora took a sip of water. "Just a little bug. Nothing serious."

Earl narrowed his eyes and leaned closer. "You see the doctor."

Propping her head on her hand, Cora said, "I am a doctor. And yes I got a second opinion and there's nothing wrong."

"Humph, never did believe anything a doctor had to say."

"Hey," Cora scolded. "You're sitting at the table with one."

"Well, you're the only doctor I trust."

Cora put out the last of the chocolate cake. "I've been meaning to ask something."

Virgil and Earl looked at her with anticipation clouding their eyes. "What?" they asked in unison.

"Carl gets his medal Saturday and I was thinking we might throw him a party. It will be quite a celebration."

Virgil smiled. "That's a good idea." His brow furrowed. "Are you sure you feel up to it?"

"I wasn't thinking of much. Maybe just sandwiches, punch and a cake."

Earl leaned back. "Why don't we do it at the church instead? We could have a potluck, a party and introduce the new Reverend Washburn. All at the same time."

Jack had been leaning against the table, resting his chin on his hands. At Earl's proposal, he piped up. "I like that idea. Then us kids can play games in the church."

Cora cocked her head to one side. "I don't want the reverend to upstage Carl. We're all pretty proud of him."

Earl put down his fork and wiped his mouth. "I won't let that happen. I'm mighty thankful for Carl, too."

"I'll let Maggie, Susan, Helen and Ester know about it and they can spread the news. That should get the ball rolling."

"You just need to tell Meredith, she's the town telegraph," Earl grumbled.

"Honestly, Earl. You pick on that woman something terrible," Cora scolded. "You make her out to be a busybody when she's very nice."

Her nephew looked up between bites. "I don't know what Earl's talking about, but the woman sure can't cook."

"Jack!" Cora was shocked that he would say something so mean. "That's not nice."

Jack shrugged. "All I know is when we had the bake sale at school a couple of weeks ago, Miss Meredith's stuff didn't get sold."

"Well, maybe she didn't bake something people liked."

Earl smiled at Jack. "She baked something. That's all it took."

Cora got up to refill her glass. "I like the woman and this table isn't a place where we criticize people."

A wave of nausea washed over Cora. As she stood to go to the bathroom the room spun and she collapsed.

CHAPTER TWENTY-FOUR

Virgil saw Cora's face pale and go completely white when she stood. He automatically reached out and caught her before she hit the floor. His heart nearly broke a rib from pounding so hard. Worried, he carried her to bed and ordered Jack to bring a wet washcloth for her forehead.

"What's wrong with her?" Earl asked, hovering over her on the opposite side of the bed. "Want me to call an ambulance?"

Cora's eyes fluttered open and Virgil felt the knot in his chest loosen. "What...what happened?"

"You fainted."

Placing the back of her hand on her forehead, she looked around the bedroom. "I've never done that before."

"I think I should take you to the hospital."

She rose up on her elbows and smiled at Jack sitting on the edge of the bed on the verge of tears. "I feel fine now, sweetheart. Don't worry. I didn't eat much today and it finally caught up with me."

"Don't tell us not to worry, young lady. If Virgil hadn't caught you, you might have woken up with a knot on your noggin," Earl griped. "What the hell kind of stomach bug could cause all that?"

"I'm fine." She lay back down. "Stop fussing over me like I'm a child." She closed her eyes. "Jack, please help Uncle Virgil with the kitchen then get ready for bed. I'm going to just close my eyes for a moment."

Virgil and Earl shared a worried glance and Cora rolled over.

"She's right. Let's get out of here so she can rest."

Back in the kitchen, Virgil hurried Earl out the door and ran through Jack's bedtime rituals. Then he returned to Cora.

Leaning over her, he watched her eyes flutter open. "Be honest. Are you sick enough to be in the hospital?"

"No," she said, pushing into a sitting position. "I actually feel fine now." She blinked several times and rubbed her stomach. "I'm even a little hungry."

"Tell me what to fix and it's yours."

"I'd actually like a burger and fries from Betty's Diner."

That surprised the hell out of him. "Are you sure?"

"Yes, I don't know why, but that's what I want."

"Okay, you stay right here in bed until I come back." He stood and walked to the door. "And this means no more complaining when Jack and I want burgers."

She smiled and he knew things were okay. "Agreed."

The next day Virgil drove her to work with the solemn promise that if she didn't feel well, she'd admit herself into the hospital and not move until he got there.

On the way to the office, Virgil realized that didn't make him feel better. Now, as he pushed through the door he wished he'd insisted she call in sick and stay home in bed.

To his surprise, Gene McKinnon stood talking to Ethan. "What brings you here this early?" he asked the FBI agent.

"I got the evidence back and it all points to the fact that Henry Ryder did indeed set fire to his own hardware store."

Virgil slumped down in an empty chair. "Damned if I didn't know it."

Shaking his head, Gene tossed a folder on Virgil's lap. "The evidence shows not only was there kerosene on the tops of his shoes, but the soles were soaked in the liquid."

Virgil looked over the evidence report. "So he walked right through that shit. He could've burned himself to death."

"No one ever claimed criminals were smart."

Virgil stood. "Ethan, stay here for a few minutes. We'll be right back." He motioned to Gene. "Let's go. This is one arrest I'm looking forward to."

They arrived at Henry's house to see him getting ready to get in his car. His hands and arms had healed enough to where they were no longer bandaged, but Virgil bet beneath those gloves they hurt like hell.

He limped to the car door then stopped when he saw them pulling up the driveway. "What the hell do you want?"

"I'm here to arrest you, Henry Ryder, for burning down your own property."

"I didn't do any such thing."

Gene put his hands in his coat and stared hard at Henry. "That's not what the evidence says."

"What evidence?"

"On your shoes," Gene continued. "You're not real smart. When you set a fire, you never pour the liquid ahead of you. It's important you walk backwards. Even Eddie's boys knew that."

"I don't know what you're talking about."

Virgil took Henry by the arm. "Come with me. We'll let the judge decide. I'm not going to shackle you because of your burns and I've no desire to hurt you, but that doesn't mean I won't."

"I'm going to get me a lawyer."

Gene looked at Virgil and smiled. "Good, because you're going to need one."

Back at the station, Gene left and Ethan went home to grab some shuteye. The last couple of weeks had been exhausting. Now, maybe they could finally catch up on their sleep.

Judge Garner came in and, for once, he was smiling. "Looks like we can bring all this arson stuff to a conclusion."

Virgil ran his fingers through his hair. "Yeah, I'm glad Gene was able to provide enough evidence to put Henry away."

The judge sat on the corner of the desk. "That Dawson guy did a great job in court laying out Eddie and Matthew's case. He knew exactly how, when, where and even the cause of those fires."

"And when I was able to get a timeline, and the statement from the kerosene delivery guy, and Eddie's bank statement, there wasn't much left to do."

"Yes, I'm sure they'll be convicted."

"You think the other boys were involved."

"Mark and Luke Summerfield?"

"Yeah."

The judge scratched his head. "There's an excellent chance they did their part. I hope after seeing what's going to happen to their father and brother, they'll be toeing the line."

"I'm just glad it's all over. At least we don't have to worry about setting the trap in the furniture store. That never did sit well with me. Too dangerous. Now, I can concentrate on shutting Dan Martin down."

"I applied to have the trial here, but I haven't heard back yet," the judge confirmed.

"As soon as Cora's feeling better I'm going to get in touch with that lawyer friend of yours."

"Wait until we see if they'll move it here." Taking his hat, the judge moved toward the door. "Did you say Cora wasn't feeling well?"

"Yeah. She's been to the doctor. I'm planning to leave in a few minutes to see how she's doing."

"Give her my regards."

At the hospital, Virgil went into Cora's office to find it empty. Knowing she'd eventually show up, he decided to wait a few minutes.

It wasn't long before she came in, looking more tired than ever. She reached down and captured his mouth in a wet kiss. "Feeling better?"

"A little."

That meant no.

"Have you checked back with the doctor?"

"I will if I'm not better tomorrow."

"You'll be happy to hear I locked up Henry today."

She smiled. "Good. That man belongs behind bars just for being so mean."

"I know, but Gene McKinnon has a pretty good case against him."

The phone rang and she held up her finger. "Hold on. I won't be long."

Virgil smiled, propped his ankle on his thigh and looked around at the nice office. Cora had done well here and was respected by most of the medical community. He couldn't be prouder.

"Yes, I understand. I will."

Cora was whiter than the coat she wore. "What is it? What's wrong?"

She stood, holding on to the desk. Tears filled her eyes and Virgil's knees nearly buckled as he reached for her. Putting her hands on his shoulders, tears coursed down her cheeks.

"You're not going to believe this."

"Try me, for Christ's sake," his voice grew louder than he intended.

"I'm pregnant."

BOOKS BY GERI FOSTER

THE FALCON SECURITIES SERIES
OUT OF THE DARK
WWW.AMAZON.COM/DP/B00CB8GY9K

OUT OF THE SHADOWS
WWW.AMAZON.COM/DP/B00CB4QY8U

OUT OF THE NIGHT
WWW.AMAZON.COM/DP/B00F1F7Q9M

OUT OF THE PAST
WWW.AMAZON.COM/DP/B00JSVTRVU

ACCIDENTAL PLEASURES SERIES

WRONG ROOM
WWW.AMAZON.COM/DP/B00GM9PU94

WRONG BRIDE
WWW.AMAZON.COM/DP/B00NOZMNSU

WRONG PLAN
WWW.AMAZON.COM/DP/B00MO2RFR8

WRONG HOLLY
WWW.AMAZON.COM/DP/B00OBS03M2
WRONG GUY
WWW.AMAZON.COM/DP/B00KK94F6G

ABOUT THE AUTHOR

As long as she can remember, Geri Foster has been a lover of reading and the written words. In the seventh grade she wore out two library cards and had read every book in her age area of the library. After raising a family and saying good-bye to the corporate world, she tried her hand at writing.

Action, intrigue, danger and sultry romance drew her like a magnet. That's why she has no choice but to write action-romance suspense. While she reads every genre under the sun, she's always been drawn to guns, bombs and fighting men. Secrecy and suspense move her to write edgy stories about daring and honorable heroes who manage against all odds to end up with their one true love.

You can contact Geri Foster at geri.foster@att.net

Made in the USA
Lexington, KY
18 July 2016